The Creatures of the Carp

The Creatures
of the Carp

written and illustrated by
Roland Portchmouth

SCOTTISH CHILDREN'S PRESS

First published in 1977
This edition printed in 1998 by
SCOTTISH CHILDREN'S PRESS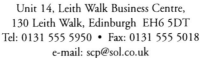

Unit 14, Leith Walk Business Centre,
130 Leith Walk, Edinburgh EH6 5DT
Tel: 0131 555 5950 • Fax: 0131 555 5018
e-mail: scp@sol.co.uk
http://www.taynet.co.uk/users/scp

text and illustrations © Roland Portchmouth, 1998

*the right of Roland Portchmouth to be identified as the Author
of this work has been asserted by him in accordance with the
Copyright, Designs and Patents Act, 1988*

Scottish Children's Press is an imprint of Scottish Cultural Press

British Library Cataloguing in Publication Data
A catalogue record for this book is available from the British Library

The publisher acknowledges subsidy from

THE SCOTTISH ARTS COUNCIL

towards the publication of this volume

ISBN: 1 899827 65 X

Printed and bound by ColourBooks Ltd, Dublin

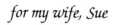

for my wife, Sue

Contents

Preface

So that you'll know something about who wrote this book, the publishers have asked me to tell you a bit about myself. But which bits? We all have so many bits to our lives. I have a wife and family and a little black cat called Pipistrelle, but should I also mention my earlier years as a sailor in the Navy; or in Art College as a student; or in schools as a teacher and lecturer; or in the church as a minister? And what of my books on art? Or my pictures and poems about animals?

One day I moved to Scotland. It was here on the mountains and moors, and among the rocks and caves of the seashore that I first encountered wild creatures in their own habitat. They were all so beautiful and wonderfully made for their way of life.

But one thing puzzled me: why did so many have to kill others in order to survive? It was so cruel – so wasteful of life and beauty! Did Nature have to be like this? As I drew more birds and animals, I began to feel a strange closeness to them. Was I becoming part of their world? This was my inspiration for *The Creatures of the Carp*, which I hope you enjoy reading.

Roland Portchmouth

I saw the wild cat crouched

It happened before the owl could shriek,
Before the fox could turn,
Before the hares of night could leap
Into the moonlit fern;
And the men who stood below the wood
Felt fear within them burn.

Extract from *The Ballad of the Mares*
by the Author

1

The Lost Mine

Far to the north, along coasts lying in the path of great gales, a line of hills turns suddenly out to sea, projecting some half mile into the heart of the grey wastes. Advancing tides divide at the headland and roll, foaming, along either side. From the top of the rounded ridge, stripped bare to the rock by wind, the slopes drop steeply over rough ground to where small stone cottages crouch for shelter underneath, just as they did before the terrifying events of this story overtook them. Perhaps not quite as they did then, for what happened changed the lives within them so that nothing was ever the same again.

Every day, from the safety of their homes, families had looked out across the long ocean swell to empty horizons and thought that they would always be able to do so. Every night, in the warmth of their beds, they had listened to the sound of the dark waves tumbling below, and had no reason to feel insecure. But if they had listened to the uneasy voice of the gull or curlew, or to the far-off dog-fox crying in the night, they would have heard the first, faint warnings that everything was not as it should be. If they had waited a little longer among the boulders and tidal pools of the shore where the grey crabs gathered, or seen up the hillside the face of the wild cat watching them, they would have sensed a fear they could not put a name to.

Events of that winter were to be overhung by more than the dark mass of the Carp outlined against the sky above them; and if those who saw strange movements there had only talked about them to others, there would have been no doubt where the danger came from. High up among the outcropping rocks it was beginning to take shape; it stirred in the deep hollows of the slopes; it brushed silently through the coarse heather, and left light footprints in the turf. Every shadow on the hill hid a blacker one inside it. Nobody could be sure what things they were that raced from cover to cover, or took off into the white, swirling mists.

But in a cosy room round blazing peat and driftwood, they would say to each other, when talking about the hill, 'There's always been goings-on on the Carp, and there always will be. No one knows what it's up to, out there by itself. By storm-light or moonlight or under a blue sky, it's never the same next time you look.'

Because the crofters had grown up with the Carp, as their ancestors had done before them, they were part of

. . . to look back towards the Carp, surrounded by the shining sea

it: they shared its changing moods and accepted that it had secrets of its own. Probably that was why no one paid much attention when the approach of that fateful winter brought an unearthly stillness to its heights.

Not that the headlanders had much time for wondering: life on the Carp saw to that. The stony earth round each cottage, ringed by low walls, gave only a few root vegetables and thin oats for all the trouble spent with spade and hoe; the sheep and goats and stray poultry found little enough among the patches of salt grass on the hillsides. The sea, it is true, never failed with full trawls of herring and shell fish when the weather was kind, but all too often, day after day of relentless storms prevented the small boats from putting out.

Between times there were nets to make and mend, sails to repair, baskets to be woven from the osiers and reeds collected on the Grettel marshes. Every so often, some of the men took traps along the top of the Carp to where it met the high lands and dropped again on the far side into larch and spruce woods. But that was as far as anyone went; beyond were the Dollom moors, trackless and desolate, home of the unknown spirits.

Sometimes boys from the crofts accompanied the trapping party. They helped with fetching home the game and furs; but Rory, one of the youngest, would often climb with them just to look back towards the Carp, surrounded by the shining sea, and feel he was like a bird, seeing it far below. He would picture to himself his sister, Ailsa, in their small house on the south slope, where they had lived alone together for as long as he remembered. He called to mind the stories that people whispered among themselves about the two orphans and about the family he had never known. Folk who had lived longest in the crofts spoke of his grandfather, Haakon Chefennec, one of five brothers who had grown up there from boys. The five were well known. There was Rognvald the basket maker; Sigurd the woodsman; Torquil the boat builder and Ingvar the carrier. The old man himself had been almost a hermit, roaming the Carp alone and learning secrets hidden from the eyes of others. Sometimes he was not seen for days, only to be spotted on the skyline returning from a journey to the inland hills. Often he took out his boat as far as the two islands that lay off the Carp Point, and spent long periods there on his own. No one knew what he did, except perhaps his brothers, to whom he had always been attached.

That the family shared his secrets became apparent finally when they were all seen together digging a deep hole near the top of the south face. Day and night they worked, sinking a shaft and extending tunnels underground. It was rumoured that they had struck a precious seam – some said of quartz, others of silver; but whichever was the case, their frequent visits with picks and shovels left no doubt that they were exploring a mine of some sort. What was curious was that the brothers never brought any ores to the surface. Whatever they collected they left in the underground gallery and as the entrance was always secured with a large iron lock, there was no chance for others to investigate.

More curious than this carefully guarded secret however, and what aroused growing suspicion over the following months, was the disappearance first of Old Chefennec himself and then of the brothers, one after the other. Those remaining said little about the disappearances, except to make mysterious reference to 'journeys inland'. In the end they also vanished, leaving behind only one son – Rory's father, Seamus, who had somehow never seemed to get on with the others. He and his wife continued on in the crofts until their daughter, Ailsa, was six or seven. Then, soon after Rory arrived, their mother died. Of their father, nothing more was ever heard again after the funeral. Neighbours searched for him and waited, wondering if he would turn up or if he too had gone for good. Finally, when no news came of the missing man, they took it on themselves to look after the two children until such time as Ailsa was old enough to manage for both of them.

As often as Rory came to this spot, his thoughts wandered back along the bleak headland of the Carp, searching for an answer to the riddle. But what puzzled him most was the end of the strange story, for it did not end with his father's going. For a long time afterwards, superstition prevented any of the crofters from venturing near the mine. Then, as memories faded and they grew less cautious, they tried to undo the great lock, but they could not shift it. Even if the ingenious mechanism had not baffled them, the rust of years made sure it would never turn again. The entrance had remained unopened until, within Rory's own memory, came the last, incredible development. One morning, the entrance to the mine was not there any more. No trace of it was to be found. The ground around was flat and unbroken, as though nothing had ever disturbed it. The fate of the mine and the Chefennec family was sealed under the silent earth.

With the whole of the Carp stretched out below, Rory tried to imagine where the shaft started and the course it may have taken underground. With his eyes shielded against the glare of the distance, he followed each winding track through gorse and bracken, looking for a tell-tale sign. But there was nothing. The bleak slopes were always the same and gave nothing away. And he would sling across his shoulder the hares or woodcock that he had been given to carry, and rejoin the rest of the party.

It was during the second month of winter that, returning from such a trip, the hunters were met at the village by great excitement. In their absence Old Maddy Obdolon had made a discovery. Too old for most jobs, Maddy was left to look after the ragged herds that browsed the steep scrub; and with little enough to do, he took the opportunity of keeping an eye open for the missing mine. Prodding around with his stick that morning, he had felt the end sink unexpectedly through soft marl, and saved himself only in time from falling into the hole that opened. At the bottom, under loose soil and flints, was lying a hidebound book, damp and stained, but with the writing inside still readable. Readable, that is, to any who could make head or tail of it, which Maddy could not. Others he took it to managed little better. Had it been straightforward they would scarcely have succeeded, for writing of any sort was much of a mystery to them; but the angular script zigzagged across the page in an almost meaningless scrawl. Words were strung together, interspersed with quaint symbols, and arranged in all directions as though the author had turned the book round frequently as he wrote.

After arguing for a while, they decided to take it to the only person in the crofts who was likely to throw any light on the matter – old Dendroger. By Carp standards, and by any other come to that, Dendroger was a scholar. His house at the foot of the north face was known to be strewn with odd volumes and papers over which he pored by the light from his small window. Through the same opening, passers-by had seen him engrossed with various experiments; but what he was up to, no one could tell. His door remained mostly shut, and he rarely came outside, so that he was regarded by his neighbours with both mistrust and awe. But with the discovery of the book, curiosity overcame their prejudice and, led by Maddy, they set off down the Carp to call on the old recluse.

The figure confronting them when the door opened would have given alarm to none save those who went in fear of hobgoblins. Bent with great age, he bobbed mechanically up and down as if trying to find the best angle from which to view his visitors. Large, pale eyes rolled from one to the other of the group, while the crinkled face toyed with expressions best suited for receiving them. Remnants of smoky hair hung about the taut scalp, but sprouted in confusion from the chin, which worked rhythmically to keep them in motion.

It took all Maddy's concentration to explain why they had come, and only from the trembling, extended hand did he gather that the old fellow had grasped the reason. Had Maddy seen the eyes fixed swiftly on the book, or noticed the stiffening of the frail body, he might have gathered even more. But how was he to know that Dendroger had been expecting the book to turn up all along, and that he could not wait to get possession of it? Feigning a show of bewilderment, Dendroger turned the covers and peered at the pages, seemingly unable to make sense of them; but under lowered lids, the glance sped rapidly from word to word and lit with concealed satisfaction. Affecting to offer little hope, he said he would do what he could.

'I'm afraid we can't expect much,' the voice shrilled. 'The language is unusual, and may be no language at all. Perhaps it's the work of a madman or a joker. I don't know. Come back in a week or so when I've had a chance to study it.'

The door closed in their faces; and seeing there was nothing more they could do about the matter, the deputation made their separate ways home up the Carp.

It towered above them in the likeness of a giant timber wolf

2

Strange Things
Start to Happen

If Old Maddy and his neighbours spent long hours discussing the book when they got home, or had cause to think about it much in the following days, all such thoughts were put out of mind by events one morning about a week later.

The red sun had barely lifted clear of the high peaks to the east when, to all ears, came a sound from the Carp that froze every action and put a stop to every conversation. In homes below the pitch of its steep sides, families stood looking at one another. Those already about some business on the slopes stared up at the ridge in the direction of the sound. Far above, silhouetted against the sky, they saw the figure, its long skirts billowing in the wind, a shawl flying and tugging from the shoulders. The woman's single scream still hung in the air, and next second a man was seen running back from further along the ridge to where she held her hands protectively before her face. As he reached her, she pointed wildly along the crest of the Carp towards the eastern hills.

Rory and other boys who had been out getting water were first on the scene. Soon, others from the lower levels joined them and crowded round. The woman, white and shaking, was trying to talk, but her eyes were fixed in wide alarm at a point on the path ahead, and her speech was broken and confused. Calming her as best he could and explaining to the rest what had happened, the man said that he and his wife were collecting bracken and dry gorse for kindling, when up the hill rushed a rabble of croft mongrels on the tail of a dog-fox.

'They cornered it on the ridge in front of Morag,' he went on, 'and were just snatching to pull it down when it rose on its haunches from under their very jaws and towered above them in the likeness of a giant timber wolf, its stiff hair flaring down its spine and eyes on fire!'

'True as I'm still alive,' the woman cut in hysterically, 'the thing rounded on the dogs that were struck dumb with terror, and the pack broke, making off all ways at once like they'd seen the Devil.'

'The brute didn't go for you?' asked Ana Guonda, wife of the blacksmith.

'It turned and was gone before I had the wit to scream,' replied Morag, now more composed, but glancing nervously about among the grey boulders, expecting one of them at any moment to change into the wolf.

A search of the out-cropping rocks revealed nothing, and as the crofters bent their way back down the slope many were vexed by the unnecessary alarm, or just shook their heads doubtfully, marvelling how some folk can see things that others can't. But those who returned to find their dogs whimpering and cowering behind a stone wall, began to think again about what had happened and felt an uneasiness that had not troubled them before.

By itself, the incident may have been taken lightly and perhaps forgotten; but when, a day or so later, Jens Shardolf put out in his boat for the fishing grounds off Carp Point, it was to lead within the hour to a graver view of matters.

Alone, as he always was, Jens took advantage of the flood tide to float his boat off the shingle, pulling strongly towards the two off-shore islands beyond which the deeper water attracted large shoals of herring. By coincidence of structure and tidal action, the islands were identical in every aspect, each rising sheer on the south side and descending by steps to the north. Where one had a prominence or jutting ledge, the second had another shaped exactly like it; where the first had a cave or cleft or scar, so did its twin. Because there was nothing to choose between them, they had become known as the Twin Jaks – a name that gave no hint of their ominous reputation.

In heavy seas, when the swell lifted and poured

through the narrow channel dividing them, rafts of oarweed were carried high on to the rocks, to be plucked off by the next wave. It was a common sight to see scores of small crabs gusted like hailstones on to the steep beach. But they were the only visitors ever seen to land there. Brooding and hostile, the grim peaks invited no one. Even the crabs, bewildered by their experience, lost no time in scuttling back into the waves, preferring another rough handling to the risk of staying on land a moment longer than necessary. Herring gulls and cormorants circled the islands but never set foot on them. Ideal though the peaks seemed, something about them made the birds wary; coming in close by chance, they would sense a strange foreboding and wheel away into the wide sea lanes beyond.

Better than anyone in the crofts, Jens knew about the Twin Jaks. To start with, no one but he took the same course past them to the herring grounds: others chose to fish further afield. But, as he saw it, the good catches to be had there were a stronger argument than the superstitious tales put about. Not that he disregarded these completely, for like everyone else, he had come to look on the islands as things apart and not to be interfered with. For that reason, he never beached the boat or moored under the shelter of their rocks. In fact, he would give them as wide a berth as possible, passing well out of reach of them on one side or the other.

As he came abreast of the North Jak and turned to let go his trawl, he caught sight of the familiar disturbance in the water that indicated the presence of a shoal.

Aware of a concentration of glinting movement just below the surface, he realised that part of the shoal had separated and risen so that he could see individual fish quite clearly. The air above filled instantly with gulls and gannets, drawn to the spot by the tell-tale sign. As he watched, one dived from almost overhead straight at a silver streak in the centre; then as the beaked head struck, without warning the slim body of the fish expanded into a black, finned form of immense size which the gannet, unable to avoid, glanced off like a ricocheting bullet and fell flapping into the waves. Torn between the two, Jens was only quick enough to see the fin of the giant fish cut a swift circle through the water and vanish into the depths as the bird feebly pulled itself away and climbed, dazed and unsteady, into the low wind.

Even as the watcher stared in disbelief at the swirl of eddies that was all to be seen, a jolt and the splintering of timbers spun him round, and the dark face of the North Jak reared above him. Helpless, he felt the small boat thrown again against the rock and then flung clear to drift, bobbing like a cork, into the open channel. The trawl had gone, dragged from the gunwhale by the sudden motion; but only too glad to find the distance lengthening between him and the island, Jens grabbed the oars and swung the boat hard on course back to the Carp.

Those on shore who had followed his frantic return waded into the surf to meet him. Rory and his friends, Callum and Padruig, were among the first but others were close behind, and between them they helped pull the damaged bow above tide level. Jens shook off the hands that offered him support and stood trembling, his eyes fixed on the point out at sea as though waiting for something to appear. In the flat tones of one in a trance he murmured, 'The North Jak was right ahead and I didn't see it. But what was it I saw? It wasn't nat'ral, not by any means it wasn't!' His loose mouth quivered, making an effort to find words, and finally he faced the group.

'It wasn't nat'ral,' he repeated dully.

'What wasn't natural?' demanded Lars Guonda, trying to make the man talk sense. The blacksmith had had enough of mysteries after his wife's account of the phantom wolf.

Jens turned on him suddenly, pulled up by the other's brusque manner.

'You'd have known if you'd seen it,' he grated, his sallow features drawn into pits of shadow. 'One minute it was a herring; next it wasn't. Came up with the shoal, then sudden-like, there wasn't a herring, but just the black brute of a shark instead.'

'Maybe it was attacking the shoal from below,' suggested another of the group.

'Not that way up, it wasn't,' Jens stated. 'Besides, I saw it. The fish changed shape under my own eyes. Then I was aground on the Jak before I knew it.'

For a moment, recollection of his boat made him turn his attention to it, and the rest, sensing they would get no more from him, went their various ways, taking their thoughts with them and wondering what really happened. Far out, the Twin Jaks looked towards the land and the waves were empty.

Talk in the crofts touched on little apart from the two stories. Those who did not know Morag for the level-headed woman she was, could certainly think of nothing in the fisherman's nature that was given to fancy. As far as recollection went, neither of them had ever imagined anything before: that both should do so in the same week was past believing. Something had happened to unbalance them. But what? The two events were linked in some fashion: in one case a fox had changed into a wolf; in the other, a herring had become a shark. Two people had witnessed the same thing take place under different circumstances and at different times. There must be a connection, but if so, what was it? Of one fact everybody was sure: there was no good in it. Whatever was working mischief on the Carp was doing so likewise out by the Twin Jaks. As Jens had said, something unnatural had come among them. Whom would it touch next?

Some began to recall odd experiences they had had themselves. At the time, they thought best not to mention them; and now when they wanted to, they could not quite remember. There was the form that had emerged from under the shingle beach and walked upright into the spray. Then there were the voices coming from a cave that contained nothing more than crabs in a tidal pool. Once, grey shapes were seen flying out of a rabbit warren on the south slope of the Carp and rising swiftly into the low evening stars.

The incidents could have been a trick of the light; but were they? Too many had happened for them all to be imagined. Perhaps nerves were getting strained. It was understandable. Ever since the disappearance of the old mine, folk had been on edge. They might have seen unusual things if they were half expecting to do so.

Not least among the speculations was that the mine itself lay at the root of the unrest; that in some way, the events of long ago still influenced the lives of those remaining. By what means the past could reach up and affect the present, none could say, but the unsolved mystery still returned to worry people's minds, especially since the discovery of the old book which Maddy Obdolon had found buried near the site. The other opinion, shared by many, was that the Twin Jaks were behind it all. The peaks had been a constant threat beyond their shores. There was something not right about them, being so like each other, and not settled by the sea birds either.

Like everyone, Rory and his sister, Ailsa, could talk of little else. In the excitement of the last few days, jobs had been overlooked, and it was late the following afternoon when Rory remembered that he had promised he would get Ailsa some reeds from the nearby marshes for making mats. While there was still light left, he set off along the south face of the Carp to where it began sloping to the Grettel marshes spread out below. The only person he met was Jens Shardolf on his way back up the north face from making his usual deliveries of shellfish. Already the sky was darkening, and a wind off the sea was gusting squalls of rain across the land ahead. Evening had come quickly to the marsh, and the grey waters of the Grettel stream gleamed dully as they broadened into the estuary. Rory followed its course a distance, passing an old dilapidated cottage that had stood there deserted for as long as he could recall, until he came to the dense reed beds that lay along either bank. Choosing the straightest he could find, he gathered as many reeds as he could carry, then turned and made his way back across the swampy flats. Through the driving rain and mists he could see the dim outlines of the Carp, still a long way off.

The rustle caused the figures to turn silently in his direction

3

Night of Terrors

In the darkness to his left, Rory heard the sound of heavy breakers on the shore and knew there was a high sea running. Night was closing in fast, and he glanced at the inky shadows round him, wishing he were nearer home; but it was some way yet to the edge of the marsh, and the ground underfoot was slippery with wet turf and mud.

It was as he entered a shadow deeper than the rest that he saw immediately ahead what at first he thought were stunted trees, forming a small coppice. Then, as he came almost up to them, something about their shape and actions made him stop. A few steps further and he realised, with heart pounding, that he would have walked straight into a circle of figures, talking quietly together. Not daring to breathe, Rory could hardly believe the sight before him. Taller than himself, the figures were making curious flapping gestures with their arms, and low trills came from among them; then a hoarse croak broke in, followed by strange growling and mewing noises – sounds that he had heard the curlew make, and the hooded crow from the estuary; sounds that he had listened to along the foreshore where the guillemots gathered, or from the skies above Dollom moor when the buzzard hung in its deadly watch. Then all at once, he knew! As he caught the shine of rain on feathers, he saw the broad, flat wings falling from the shoulders of the figures, and the beaked faces moving slowly up and down as the creatures spoke among themselves.

Sensing that he was as much in view as they were, he tried cautiously to melt back into the gloom behind; but in doing so, he let some reeds slip from the bundle under his arms, and the rustle as they fell caused the figures to turn silently in his direction. Their eyes, masked by the dark, fixed on him for a moment; then, with one accord, they stretched out their wings tip to tip, presenting a barrier across the path. But were they wings or the flowing sleeves of gowns? He could not be sure: they fluttered and rippled in a way that either would. And below them was only shadow, stirring like long, draped garments in the wind. Rory forced himself to raise his eyes to meet theirs again, but even as he did so, the heads lowered and turned away. The figures, dipping their wings, wheeled into the darkness behind, and with lengthening hops and strides, made off towards the open marsh. One by one they took slowly to the air and rose on a soft rush of sound into the slanting rain. The shafts of silver parted to let them through and closed again after them, quivering against the black night. Peering to catch a last glimpse of the outlines as they faded, Rory found himself trembling and cold. He could still not believe what had taken place in front of him, or that the unearthly beings had not set upon him. One minute, they seemed to bar his way with their wings outspread; the next, they had taken flight and vanished! What kind of creatures were abroad on the marsh that night? Would they be waiting for him further along the path? Last time they had been taken by surprise at seeing him: now they would be expecting him and would be prepared.

Almost without thinking, he stooped to gather up the fallen reeds and started for home, stumbling and sliding in his haste, and hurrying past vague shapes that loomed out of the dark alongside. The image of the weird assembly came again and again to his mind, sometimes confused and blurred, so that the forms were neither of men or birds, sometimes clearer, so that they were one or the other. Had they been real, or had he imagined them? No bird was the size that these were, that was certain; but then, no man was mantled with wings or given to flying off as these had done. What did it all mean? Was he starting to see things that were not there, just as some people said that Morag and Jens had? Or had he, like them, been drawn into some mysterious world quite different from the one they all knew?

From far away on the marsh came the shriek of a

snowy owl, and Rory took hold of himself, pushing on all the faster. Then, from somewhere closer, a voice cried out, but pausing and hearing nothing more, he remembered the harsh, almost human note of the bittern, and reassured himself with the thought of the hidden nest nearby among the rushes. Was there a simple explanation also for the other things that had happened? Perhaps when he told Ailsa, she would be able to explain them. As soon as he got home he would tell her everything. But would she believe him? He could hardly believe himself that he had not been dreaming.

Although the lamp at the cottage window was in sight above him on the hill, it was to be some hours, as it turned out, before he could tell Ailsa his story. The weather had been worsening steadily and, on the more exposed incline, broke on him with a suddenness that took his breath away. Full in the path of the storm, the Carp was all but lost under driving sheets of rain that danced and raced up the steep slope before the following wind. Out to sea, gigantic swells lifted towards the shore, and burst in flying spray upon the rocks.

As Rory beat his way up the track leading to the house, he saw with surprise that the door was blowing open and shut. On any night it would have been strange to find the door off the latch, but on one such as this he could not understand it, and was seized with alarm for Ailsa's safety. Inside, curtains flapped and cupboards banged, and an air of desolation hung over the half-laid table. There was no sign of his sister and, throwing down his bundle, he ran outside again to search the low-walled paddock and outbuildings. About to call her name, he became aware at the same instant of a crowd of people further up the slope, sheltering from the storm behind the high beached hunter boat. Hurrying to the higher level where they were talking excitedly together, he found Ailsa among them. As he clutched her arm, she turned with an expression of relief at seeing him; then, pointing to a spot out to sea beyond the headland, she shouted to make her words heard above the wind.

'The Twin Jaks, Rory, the Twin Jaks! Something's happening out there !'

He shielded his eyes to follow the direction she indicated, where the two islands stood beyond the streaming spray and rain, their pinnacles etched black against the deafening and birdless night. At first glance, Rory could detect nothing unusual, then all at once, and thinking he had taken leave of his senses, he saw what the others had been watching. Almost blinded by the stinging salt, he stared wide-eyed as, slowly, by almost imperceptible degrees, one of the Jaks was turning round. He blinked, and blinked again, convinced he had imagined it. But no, there was no doubt! Like the hull of a great ship swinging at anchor, the south island was completing a half circle and coming to rest facing the opposite direction. In its new position, it seemed no longer to repeat the outline of the other as before, but to mirror it instead, confronting its own image in a glass.

Nothing about the spectacle was so awesome and unnerving as the smooth ease with which it was accomplished, as though a piece of heavy, oiled machinery had revolved, locking precisely into place. Then everything was exactly as it had been a moment earlier – the peaks braced against the mountainous Atlantic that reared and fell past them, foaming and thundering towards the shore. To a stranger not familiar with the Jaks, nothing would have seemed changed; but the frightened group drawn close together on the hillside were struck by the immensity of the power that could have brought this thing about, by the dark force that moved under the waters. Three times now it had shown its hand. Three unexplainable events had left their mark on every heart. Rory alone among the shivering, huddled group, knew of yet another that would have deepened their fear further.

As his recent encounter on the marsh flashed to mind, an urgent need to talk to Ailsa about it made him take her arm and steer her away from the rest; and, leaving them to make what they could of the mystery surrounding the island, he led her back down the winding path to their cottage. Once safe out of the tormented night, they shut and bolted the door and stood, breathless, looking at each other.

The silence still shook with tremors of what had just passed, and the dim form of the island so over-hung the small room that Rory could not free himself of the recollection. His own story seemed suddenly unimportant compared with the new threat that had sprung from the raging sea; and as he started to recount it to Ailsa, he felt as if he were telling her about a dream he had had. But the older girl quickened as she listened to him, and pressed him to try and remember as much as he could. Far from taking lightly what he said, or dismissing it as fancy, her eyes brightened with interest and she appeared to read into his words more sense than he could make of them himself. From time to time she frowned as though something in the story puzzled her, but she did not attempt to interrupt him. At the end she drew him down on to the bench to sit beside her. Rory sensed her expression soften, but the nervous tightening of her clasped hands did not escape his notice.

'Rory,' she said, an unusual tenseness in her voice, 'I don't know what's going on, or what these strange things mean, but for some reason that I can't explain now, I'm sure that they concern you and me more than anyone else in the crofts. What has happened so far is only just a beginning. Very soon we may find ourselves in great danger. So from now on, please take care. Keep close to the house after dark, and if anything like this happens again, come at once and tell me. There may be nothing we can do, but it's best to be on guard.'

His sister's earnestness alarmed Rory, and he did not know quite how to take it. However, he gave her the promise she asked for, and when she got up to prepare their evening meal, he busied himself about the room helping her. Later, over the hot vegetable broth, they tried to talk of different matters, but neither could put aside the other thoughts that kept returning.

Throughout the night torrential rain, lashed by the wind, beat down on the roof; wild surges tore at the slates and ran moaning between the low rafters like demons searching out those who sheltered underneath. At times, the building rocked before a blast, with every sign of being hurled from its foundations and carried into the whirling spaces of the sky. Up and down the Carp, families lay sleepless, listening to the dark fury raging overhead, and dreading what spectral rider was astride the elements, roaming the hill unseen and terrible, waiting to strike again at the helpless crofts. All who lay awake thought back to the events of the past days, seeing once more, in a shadowy alcove or by a curtained door, the grey shape of Morag's wolf, and the strained face of Jens Shardolf returning from the sea, and the island slowly turning through the black waters off Carp Point.

With the grey advance of morning, the storm began to ease and the rain slackened. By sunrise, the Carp lay still and shining in the golden light. Folk were astir and out early, glad that the night was over and wondering what the new day would bring. But for the time being, the skies were blue, bright clouds blew in from across the sea, and gorse sparkled on the hill. Indoors and out, there were jobs to be done after the storm, and neighbours chatted cheerfully whenever they met, comforted by the thought that yesterday's troubles had at least brought no harm to themselves and their children. Only those who glanced seawards now and then were reminded by the unfamiliar position of the South Jak that everything was not quite as it should be on the Carp.

4

The Book of Mystic Transformations

Although in the past days fear had taken hold of the crofts, and hearts raced at any unusual sight or sound, Dendroger's door had remained closed against all that happened. While on the Carp, events of the natural world were being tampered with and timeless laws thrown into confusion, Dendroger stayed bent over the old book that had been found, engrossed in unravelling its strange writing.

At first the going had been difficult, but gradually, as he became used to the short statements, tangled with diagrams and ciphers and wavering columns of calculation, he read more quickly. What unfolded before his eyes was the record of an amazing enquiry into the natural processes that governed plant and animal life on the Carp. The writer had investigated every nook and cranny, uncovering mysteries too small to be discerned and too vast to comprehend. Indefatigably, he had carried his research into the most minute cell formations and into the most sweeping laws that bound all living things together.

The discovery of the book itself the week before had not surprised the old scholar, but as he neared the end of his translation, he could hardly believe the evidence before him and sat for a while, stunned by all that it implied. Never had he seen facts so patiently collected, or complex reasoning dove-tailed with such mastery into breathtaking simplicity. With only the last few pages to go, he knew that he had stumbled on a revelation beyond the wildest dreams of men. Unsupported by its scientific proofs, the whole fabric would have seemed a fantasy. Yet it was true. In his hands was the key to a knowledge that made him tremble with the thought of it.

Realising the need to keep cool and control his mounting excitement, he read through the manuscript again. Under the heading *Rubric of Mystic Transformations* it went on:

As a result of certain experiments conducted on and around the Carp, it has been proved beyond doubt that Man has a faculty of which he is totally unaware – a faculty beyond any known to science. Records kept during these experiments are preserved herein for any who can read and understand them. To prove for himself that this faculty exists, the reader must, however, take the final step alone.

Among the wildlife of the Carp, there are only two kinds of creature – the hunter and the hunted, though the hunter, in his own turn, becomes the prey of others. In order for one species to live, it must kill another. This is the underlying rule of all creation; but I do not believe that this was originally intended. It is unbelievable that life should go to such lengths creating beauty only to have it cruelly destroyed. I decided, therefore, to follow the journey of each creature from birth, to see if I could discover what inborn weaknesses led to its downfall.

I began by observing, as far as possible, the growing embryos of all manner of marine life around the shores of the Carp, then of the land and airborne creatures that live upon it, and lastly of those that tunnel through perpetual night underground. The search covered wide expanses between the flood and ebb tides and the greater depths of water beyond; it explored rocks at the sea's threshold, where molluscs scour the green algae, and rocks above the sea's reach, where the gull and cormorant nest; it took me to the high crags of the Carp and into its ferny gulleys; it led under the earth below roots and tubers. Everywhere, I followed step by step the progress of the embryo from its infancy to its final adult form. For many, the journey ended before this point was attained, and they fell early to the jaws of predators. Others survived into maturity for varying periods until they too met a similar end.

I next examined shells above and below tide level: first, those with the living organism still in them, then those from which it was separating, and lastly those retaining only traces of occupation. I watched raiders at work, gaining entry – in turn, by the suction of starred tentacles, by the insertion of a razor claw, and by various pecking actions. More subtle deceptions for inducing the soft body to expose itself were also noted.

All these observations were accompanied in the text by detailed mathematical figures and illustrations. They continued:

> In the study of life-and-death patterns among more advanced forms, I tracked the scent trail laid across the night by the ghost moth, and counted its wing pulse; then timed the arrival on the scene of the blind bat to within a split second from the first alerted quiver of the membrane to its scything arc, cutting the insect down in flight. Hard upon this, I saw the wild cat crouched on a low branch and measured the degrees of tension that triggered it to take the bat on its returning circle.
>
> Elsewhere, I calculated the fractional movement that betrayed a grasshopper in the turf, and caught the same movement reflected in a bird's eye; then saw the snake's coil tighten and release it like an arrow at the bird.
>
> I tuned in to the heartbeat of a leveret when the scent of vixen threw the beat out of time and confused the young creature's sense of direction, leaving it paralysed in the middle of a moonlit field.
>
> Under the waters of the Grettel stream, I recorded the frequency of impulses transmitted by a trout's sudden dive, weighing them against those caused by an otter's paddle strokes, and was able to judge the exact moment of interception.

Once again, these and further findings were backed by all the proof a scholar needed. The text went on:

> Each species is equipped for living in its own special zone of one of the elements, and has come to be hunted by those in other zones. They pursue it throughout life until

The scent of vixen threw the heart-beat out of time

its escape mechanism fails, which must always happen in the end since the mechanism is designed to be slightly less efficient than that of the pursuer. As long as one kind of creature is inferior in this way and is confined to one zone, nothing will ever change.

The answer simply is that each must be able to alter shape to function as the others do, so that it can move anywhere in any element. A form capable of this would be unlike any known at present: it could take on the likeness of other creatures without being trapped within their life cycles and ending a victim as they do. If all life had this single form and mobility, none would have anything to gain by robbing another, but all would learn to subsist on the abundance of natural minerals in the universe.

Now followed the most startling part of the narrative:

The lower creatures cannot, by themselves, break from the present order. They are not born with the will to live beyond a certain time, but only to reproduce copies of themselves that will suffer a fate identical to their's later. Only man can conceive the kind of form that could adjust to infinite changes and strike the subtle balance of structures for slipping in and out of elements as he chooses. For the process is not merely a physical one: it is born of creative sources deep within him, and perfected by psychic energy.

From my experiments on the Carp, I knew that discovery lay almost within reach; but here I could only go so far. Some instinct told me that the final solution lay further away; and, crossing on to the Dollom moors, I found myself drawn to a spot where two giant stones stood. After a while, I picked up voices in the silence, and heard them talk of the ancient race that had erected the stones to mark the centre of their world. But their world was not as we know it: it was an empire of space. For, by a science more advanced than ours, they had long ago discovered the secret for which I was looking, and had taken on the identity of all creatures, passing beyond the restraint of any single form.

They were all around me in the shapes of the moor, of that I was sure; but they melted into air and stream, and vanished among rocks before I could see them. This was their defence. They can only reveal themselves when all living forms are like them.

With what I learned, I was able to return to the Carp and complete what I had started, and can now enter into the world of any creature, adapting my own form to seem like others in it for the time needed.

This is only the start. As more become ready, I shall pass on the knowledge down the descending orders of the different species. The process is difficult, but for those prepared to take this step, directions are set out below. They will be clear only to an advanced intelligence who can follow them without blundering, for to make one mistake is fatal.

The graphs, equations and formulae that filled the next pages were indeed complicated. All night, Dendroger wrestled with them, but by the first light of dawn, everything fitted together and he knew he could carry out the experiment himself.

The closing section of the book, however, remained a mystery, and try as he would, he could not understand it. It seemed to have no bearing on the main experiment and to add nothing to the complete instructions already given; so dismissing it for the time being, he set about preparing to make the test.

It was on the day that was to end in the great storm and the changing round of the South Jak. The few crofters who came near Dendroger's cottage saw the window curtained and spirals of intense white smoke rising from the chimney, bearing with them floating fragments of a silvery material. Those who watched long enough, saw the smoke change colour several times and become in turn green, blue and black, matching the sea, the sky and the dark hill. But no one thought much of it, for he was a queer one, this Dendroger!

By evening, all passers-by had been driven indoors by the increasingly bad weather, and there was no witness of the shadowy figure that crept out and made its way along the foot of the Carp: no one saw the figure stoop among the rock pools and gather something in his hands; nor climb the slope and fumble in the heather; nor slip into a hollow and reappear further along the hill. Unobserved, the furtive loiterer returned home and, behind the locked door, assembled what he had collected into a curious arrangement by the hearth. Then, standing over it, he stepped briskly forward into the dense clouds of smoke that began pouring from the fire, and in a moment, was lost among its shadows.

During the next hour, anyone braving the storm may have noticed a smoky shape moving under the waves along the shore, or been startled by it as it rose from the water and winged its way up the Carp like a ghostly bird; he would have been relieved, perhaps, to see it glide earthwards and vanish down a steep burrow. But he would not have seen inside the firelit room where it slowly took shape again as the old man, smiling and apparently very pleased at the progress he was making.

With the knowledge that Dendroger now possessed, he had the power to do anything he wished. He could control what happened in the crofts and order all events to suit himself. It gave him authority over everyone living there, and over every living thing – not just on the Carp, but far beyond it; authority perhaps over the whole world. The prospect was one of infinite satisfaction to him, and into his eyes came the light of a deadly and unscrupulous ambition.

Later that night, when the villagers all stood watching aghast as the South Jak began to move, they did not see the dark form watching from the other side of the headland, also engrossed in the mysterious occurrence.

The following morning, there was nothing outside Dendroger's house to give any cause for suspicion. The curtains were drawn back from the window, and the grey smoke from the chimney was no different from that of others on the Carp. Inside, however, the master was once more deep in his study of the old book. Having successfully completed the experiment he set out to do, he was trying yet again to make sense of the last inscrutable chapter. It was not until two days later, with a sense of feverish excitement, that he realised he had finally done it.

What it proposed surpassed anything that had gone

before. Its boldness made Dendroger shrink as from a sudden fierce heat, then turn as quickly cold in the presence of an icy dread. In language even more obscure than the rest of the book, it carried the narrative beyond the earlier experiment into another, too fearful to contemplate.

As long as there are forces that can destroy all life, there is no final gain in possessing the power to live as other creatures do. These destroying forces exist in fire, in ice, and in the crushing pressures at depths below which we live. Only by overcoming these is life permanently secure.

There is one thing that has come through all these dangers without losing its identity. It has survived the molten infernos of the inner earth, the grip of glaciers, and the imponderable weight of oceans and continents on its back. With others of its kind, it has travelled down five hundred million years, and lies now below the Carp.

After months of tunnelling, we found it. In a deep gallery formed by the arched roots of a buried coal forest, we came across the fossil trilobite. The small creature was pressed into rock, looking exactly as it did when it scavenged the floors of the primeval ocean. Although pursued and waylaid at every turn by the great destroyers, it emerged from the abyss of time complete and unharmed; except that, without the knowledge that we now have, it was not prepared for the journey and lost its life on the way.

This need not have happened.

Locked within it, is the secret of resisting fire and ice and the weight of the earth: this is all we need to know in order to be sure of immortality. We therefore propose to step into the identity of the fossil, as we can of any creature, and make the journey back to the beginning. We shall be safe within its shield. Then, prepared by our greater knowledge, we will return across the path of each of the destroyers, but this time arrive in the present alive and beyond the power of any further agency to injure us.

The first shock had worn off, and Dendroger was strangely calm. So that was the purpose of the mine! And only he knew the awful treasure that lay underground. The secret of eternal life could be his for the finding. But how was he to get it? What he had already accomplished he had done alone, but for this final step he would need help in locating the mine shaft and bringing up what was down there.

Whom could he trust in the crofts to tackle the job? It would be difficult and dangerous and would have to be done in complete secrecy. They would have to be too slow-witted to question his real motives, but eager enough to get something from it for themselves. Only a promise of great reward would secure their co-operation and silence.

After a long time in thought, he got up and prepared to make two calls: one, on Lars Guonda the blacksmith, and his wife Ana; the other on Jens Shardolf, who fished for herring and crab off Carp Point. What he planned to offer them in exchange for their services was nothing less than to share the secrets of the book; but not, he smiled to himself, in the way that they might have hoped for!

5

Message from the Sky

In the days following the storm, while Dendroger, unknown to anyone, was preparing for the last stage of his experiments, Rory, along with his neighbours, was making good the damage that the storm had caused. Several slates on the roof had to be re-hung, window shutters repaired and fences mended. The peat store at the side of the house had blown down and had to be re-built. The weather remained fine, and nothing further happened to disturb the calm of the crofts. On the fourth morning, a brisk wind was blowing off the sea, and Rory went down to the beach to collect what driftwood he could find for the fire. Such winds always brought ashore odd lengths, thrown overboard from passing ships, or branches carried from the wooded coastline farther south.

The ebb tide had left a stretch of shingle clear and,

crumpled at the edge of the waves, he noticed a piece of frayed cloth, still wet from the sea. Drawn by its bright colours, he knelt and spread it out flat. As far as he could make out, it was a flag of some sort. Against a background that had once been the blue of mussel shells, but was now faded, appeared the outline of an eagle, embroidered in gold thread. The wings were raised as if in the act of taking flight, and Rory was reminded, with a quick shudder, of similarly poised wings that he had seen on the marsh some nights before. But this was just a pattern, and nothing to be afraid of. Besides, it was beautiful. He had never held such a thing before, although he had seen flags with different emblems on, flown from mastheads out at sea. He wondered if some ship had been wrecked in the night and the ensign torn from it as it foundered. But there was no sign of other wreckage or of any vessel in distress.

Returning home, he laid it out to dry in the sun, and as it did so, the wind caught its light folds and rippled them.

'In the sky,' he thought to himself, 'it would fly like a bird!' and he looked up at the clouds sweeping high above the Carp.

For the next few hours, he worked on his idea. Finding two slender sticks, he tied them together in the form of a cross and, with the help of Ailsa who was watching with amused interest, he stitched the cloth to them so that it was tight across the simple framework. With the end of a long reel of yarn secured to the struts, he lifted the kite above his head and felt it tug and pull as gusts seized it.

'I'll take it on to the ridge,' he called to Ailsa, hardly waiting to wave goodbye. Regretting that none of the other boys from the crofts were around to come with him and join the fun, he climbed the steep slope behind the house and stood at the top, clutching the kite that threatened to be whipped away at any second by the fast wind. Let go, it leapt into the racing heavens, snatching the limp line taut. Higher and higher it went, straining at the lengthening anchor that held it to earth, as though a great fish had taken a cast and was surging seawards with it.

Rory struggled to keep hold: he had never felt strength like this. The pull of the distant kite jerked him forward, and he found himself stumbling along the ridge, tripping on stones and tangled by gorse and thistles as he ran. With eyes only for the dancing shape above, he was brought up sharply by the stump of an old tree that stood in his path. Flinging his arms around the trunk, he made to turn the string about it; but, glancing up, noticed that it had gently slackened. It was pulling no more! Following the line of the curve upwards, he watched in stunned amazement at what was happening in the sky. The kite, far above, seemed slowly to unfold vast wings as the gold design of the eagle took bodily form and lifted clear of the cloth. Ponderously the great bird rose into the sun and veering, made course for the hills inland, disappearing finally among their clouded peaks.

The kite seemed slowly to unfold vast wings

Unable to take his eyes off the spot where the plain square of cloth hung momentarily in the wind, Rory saw it start to fall as though released by what had held it there; then, caught by a sudden up-draught, it shot skywards, snapping the line, and was swept back along the Carp to plunge over the north slope and vanish from sight. With both the kite and line gone, Rory remained motionless for some minutes, staring first after them, then at the far range of hills, trying to make out what had happened. Again, some strange influence was at work and had crossed his path. He was afraid, excited and confused; alone with only the empty sky above him.

But was it empty? Against the expanse of deep blue, a small flake of paler blue was floating back to earth, drifting and fluttering towards him. Like a feather, it came to rest in the coarse grass a short distance down the hill; and, running to pick it up, he recognised it as a corner of his kite. To his astonishment he saw that since last it was in his hands, it had been covered with angular, spidery writing, apparently drawn in liquid silk. The writing shone in the sun, but was difficult to read, and he at once thought of Ailsa. She would understand it: he would take it home and show her.

So, with the scrap of cloth safe inside his jacket, he cut back along the ridge, hoping, as he went, that he might be able to spot his kite somewhere below on the north slope in the direction where he had seen it come down. So busy was he keeping an eye open for any sign, that he did not see the three figures approaching along the ridge. Ana Guonda, with her husband and Jens

Shardolf, stopped at the top of the track they were about to take down the north slope, and waited for him to come up to them. Rory noticed that each was carrying something. Ana clasped a white hen under her cloak; her husband, Lars, had a stoat in a string bag; and Jens held a wicker cage containing a large crab.

'You'll be over the edge if you don't look where you're going,' remarked Ana, smiling in the twisted way she had. 'We thought we saw you flying a kite, but were too far away to be sure. Have you lost it down the north slope?'

Rory saw no reason for keeping back any part of the story, especially as the three already knew about the unusual things that had taken place on the Carp. He told them how he found the flag with the eagle design on, and how the kite that he made from it had come to life as a real bird in the sky. With a flush of embarrassment, he caught the amused smile that the others exchanged between themselves, implying clearly that they thought he had made up the story, probably in order to have something to boast about. He was annoyed and angry with them, wishing now that he had said nothing, and without delaying further, he brushed past and scrambled down the opposite slope on to the path that led home.

Ailsa was in the garden, lifting cabbages from the rough ground. She noticed at once his wild state, and that the kite was missing. Guessing that this was no ordinary accident, she hurried inside with him and closed the door. Once more, as on the night of the storm, Rory felt that the action shut out the mysterious presence that haunted the Carp; but this time, he had brought some small part of it back indoors with him!

Doubtful whether Ailsa was believing the fantastic story as he told it to her, he was glad to have the evidence to show; and eagerly they studied together the curious writing on the square of cloth. When, after some trouble, Ailsa managed to make out what it said, they looked at each other in bewilderment. There seemed no sense in the words, and thinking she may have misread them, Ailsa repeated them again slowly:

> The great bird is above the world and watches.
> The old tree stretches up to the bird,
> But the tree is bent and twisted under white leaves.
> If it goes underground, it will surely die.
> The youngest will find,
> But the oldest will know.

'I don't understand,' said the girl. 'Are you sure this is what came down from the sky? Do you think you might have mistaken where it landed and found this piece of cloth by accident?'

Rory was quite sure there was no mistake, and said as much. He had not taken his eyes off the object all the time it was floating to earth, and there had been nothing else lying on the bare hill top.

Ailsa stood, fingering the pale blue remnant.

'Perhaps there's a clue in these lines,' she murmured, 'if only we could find it. They must contain a message of some kind. But what's the good of a message that doesn't make sense? Maybe if we leave it for a while, an idea will come to us. I've a feeling there's something in it I ought to know, although I can't place it yet.'

Then, with exaggerated briskness, she changed the subject and added, 'I must clean and salt these cabbages, and then tidy the kitchen. You clear out the fire and make it up ready for this evening. Sometimes a problem solves itself if you stop thinking about it.'

With that, they each set about their respective jobs, Ailsa with much splashing at the sink, and Rory shovelling the ashes from the hearth; but as he idly picked from them the half-charred sticks that would do for another kindling, his thoughts drifted back to the episode of the kite, and again in his imagination he saw the great bird stepping off it into the wind and flying away.

Suddenly, Ailsa was at his side.

'I think I see,' she cried, her eyes strangely bright. 'You have to take this to someone who knows what it means. There's only one person it could refer to. Take the cloth, Rory, and go to see old Dendroger on the north side of the Carp. Show it to him. It's still early evening, you can be there and back before it gets dark. But be sure and return as soon as possible. You mustn't be out again on the Carp at night.'

Rory had no idea what his sister was talking about; and from the way she thrust the square of cloth into one hand and a large scone into the other, hurrying him out of the house, he had a feeling that she would not explain, even if he stayed to find out. Curious as to why she should suddenly think of Dendroger, he would have to wait until he got back before he could ask her.

In Dendroger's house, the old man confronted the three visitors he had furtively admitted. Lars Guonda, surly and suspicious, stood beside his wife, Ana, whose eyes gleamed with curiosity. Jens Shardolf shifted from one foot to the other, waiting nervously to hear why they had been asked to call. Choosing his words carefully, their host stressed the need for utmost secrecy in all he had to say, and looked at each in turn as if to unite them in an affair that they alone were privileged to take part in. Giving no hint of the successful experiments he had already carried out, he confided in them merely that he had at last managed to translate the old book that Maddy Obdolon had found.

'The information it contains,' he said, craning close in an air of deep conspiracy, 'is for our ears only. It's too important to share with anyone else. By following the advice in this book,' (and here he patted the volume in his hands), 'we can change ourselves into any creature we like. We could go anywhere on earth and in the sky; we could live in the ocean and the rivers as freely as the creatures who belong there.'

'But why should we want to?' asked Ana, at a loss what to make of the odd proposal.

'Because with such power, the world would be ours,'

wheezed Dendroger. 'And what's more, as there's no end to this power once we have it, we can go on living for ever, moving from one form of life to another, taking whatever shape we wish.'

He studied their reactions with cunning to see if his enticements were having the effect he wanted. The interested glances that passed between them told him that he was succeeding.

'What do we have to do?' questioned Lars, certain that there was a catch somewhere.

'We must get a creature of the earth, the air and the sea, and speak to them simply in the language they use among themselves. That's why I asked you to bring the ones you have with you. In a minute I'll show you what to say. Afterwards,' he continued, putting all his trust in their superstitious nature and their crude belief in magic, 'we must find a certain fossil shaped like a shoe from the old mine, and recite a spell over it according to the instructions in the book. Then we'll be ready for the experiment.'

'But the entrance to the mine is lost,' objected Jens Shardolf.

'There was a second entrance that no one knew about,' the old schemer smiled. 'It was on the off-shore islands. An enemy, seeing that I was on the point of solving the mystery, would try to conceal it, wouldn't he? When the South Jak was moved on the night of the storm, I put two and two together and decided that the place to look was under the side that had turned around. That's why I invited Jens to join us. He knows the waters out there and can take us. You, Lars, as you're a blacksmith, can deal with the lock which is bound to be on the door. And you, Ana, can help us search for the fossil. There's only one of its kind, and it will need a keen eye to spot it.'

Sure now that he had won their interest, he set about carrying out the farce that he had contrived, to make them think they were all starting the venture together, and that he was acting in good faith.

6

Conspiracy below the Carp

Rory followed the high ridge of the Carp to where it led down to Dendroger's house. The sea gleamed in the bronzed evening light. Against its glow, the Twin Jaks stood out darkly, silent and forbidding as ever. When he reached the old man's door, he found it shut as usual; but from behind it came sounds that he could not put a name to.

He banged hard with the flat of his hand. As the chorus inside continued and no one answered his knock, he lifted the latch and pushed open the heavy door. What he saw inside made him step back in amazement.

Dendroger, no longer frail and hunched as Rory knew him, was striding up and down, his eyes closed. Lars Guonda and Ana his wife were standing face to face

All four were completely absorbed in what they were doing

in the centre of the room, uttering strange noises in their throats such as a stoat and a hen would make. Under a small window, Jens Shardolf was propelling himself around the floor by means of arms and legs in the fashion of a crab. All four were completely absorbed in what they were doing, and it was only on retracing his steps that Dendroger opened his eyes and came up against his visitor.

'My boy!' he exclaimed delightedly. 'Come in, come in.'

He took Rory by the arm and drew him through the doorway. The others had frozen in the middle of their pantomime and were staring at him in annoyance and displeasure.

'Ailsa said I should come and see you,' he said hesitantly.

'Quite right, quite right!' the old man beamed. 'And you've come at just the right time. It's astonishing how things are working out.'

To Rory's way of thinking, his arrival was the least astonishing part of the business, and he could have explained it far more easily than what was going on around. Dendroger led him to the side of the room where, on a low hearth, was strewn an odd assortment of objects. Parts of an old sea groyne, crusted white with barnacle colonies, lay beside curiously shaped driftwood, gouged into labyrinths of tunnels by marine worms; bleached bones of gulls were erected like delicate architecture among a careful arrangement of feathers; mussel and oyster shells, piled one above the other, all showed signs of being still occupied; here and there was the black egg-case of a skate, almost hidden in a tangle of bladder-wrack, its blisters plump and wet as though fresh from the waves. And shambling knee-deep in the debris, a large crab swung its claws idly this way and that, as unconcerned as if the tide flowed over it.

But what caught Rory's eye was the framework of wood covered with cloth, a small square torn from the corner and matching the one in his hand. Something else was missing from the kite though. At first, he could not make out what it was; then suddenly he knew – the design of the eagle. It had vanished from the pale blue background without a trace.

He was on his knees in a moment to examine it closer, when he felt Dendroger's touch on his shoulder, and turning, saw the wrinkled smile above him.

'In a little while, my boy,' the thin voice was saying. 'Wouldn't you like to tell us what you called about? Was it about your kite, by any chance?'

Rory got up, aware that for some reason the room had become unaccountably quiet, and that there was growing menace in the expressions of the other three. What had he interrupted? With alarm, he met the old man's smile fixed intently on him, and felt something strangely sinister about it. He glanced aside at the beamed door, only to see that it was now secured with a lock of unusual size and complexity. His eyes slipped instinctively to where the blacksmith was standing, erect and immensely strong, his big arms loose at his sides. He knew that the lock was the smith's handiwork.

Rory could not understand what was going on. He longed to be outside on the path leading back up the Carp. But at once Dendroger was speaking again.

'Don't be frightened, boy. Show me what you have brought with you.'

There was a new harshness in the tone, as the figure before him suddenly dropped the pretence of friendliness. Why were they all looking at him and questioning him like this? Did they think he was spying on them or hiding something? His thoughts went quickly from the kite on the floor to the square of cloth he was holding. Perhaps that was what they wanted. But why should they? The kite was his in the first place, and they had no right to it. They must have found it on the north slope.

All at once, he felt a surge of anger that made him resolve to say nothing about why he had come. Wildly, he tried to think of other reasons he could give for being there. Then without warning, Dendroger seized his wrist and began prising open his fingers. In desperation, he tightened his grip and attempted to wrench free; but Lars came up and held him while the old man took the crumpled scrap and smoothed it out. Resentment blazed in him as he looked helplessly on.

Jens Shardolf, meanwhile, had picked up the crab and was fondling it like a kitten in his large, raw hands. The creature offered no resistance, but lay with its palp throbbing almost imperceptibly and its eyes rotating. The fisherman came closer and Rory watched, mesmerised, as the caressing finger traced patterns across the dark blue hairs of the mailed back. The repeating rhythm wove a drowsiness about him that he tried to shake off. Moment by moment, he was falling under the spell of the slow, circling movement, until he could do no more than follow it mechanically. From under the horny plate, pendulous claws searched out towards him, drew back into the black mouth, and extended again. Gradually his mind clouded with the blur of images; and through them came the voice of Dendroger declaiming the lines that Ailsa had read out earlier:

The great bird is above the world and watches.
The old tree stretches up to the bird,
But the tree is bent and twisted under white leaves.
If it goes underground, it will surely die.
The youngest will find
But the oldest will know.

There was a pause, then the same voice broke in again.

'Boy, is this all? Is there no more?'

Rory heard himself answer, 'That's all. There's no more.'

A curse rattled on the old lips, and the four shadowy figures moved together to the far end of the room, leaving him standing alone. As though in a trance, he saw the crab, its body held high, glide swiftly towards him from where Jens had put it down. But the coma into which he was slipping overcame him and he sank to the floor, drifting downwards into its green depths. Swayed by the long tides washing overhead, he listened to the roar and hiss as they passed. Down and down he was drawn through floating forms that crowded round and slid away again. Then there were faces peering at him, distorted by the quivering currents – nebulous faces, fringed with weeds; mouths that opened and shut like dog-fish in a trawl, releasing streams of bubbles that burst about him. And slowly the bubbles took shape as words, indistinct at first, then clearer. There was a confusion of voices, with Dendroger's rising shrilly above the rest. Every so often, the listener could make out his own name and, by degrees, what was being said. He lay, pretending still to be in a faint.

'It's just a boy's trick,' Ana was saying. 'If you ask me, I think he made up this nonsense himself.'

'He did not make it up,' replied Dendroger. 'There are things in it which he couldn't have known, though part of it was clear to Ailsa, or she'd not have sent him to see me.'

Rory's heart quickened as he heard his sister's name, and he strained to catch the next words.

'In Ailsa's eyes, I'm the one who's bent and twisted under white leaves – old Dendroger. I'm the old tree that the lines speak of, the 'oldest who will know'. Even she saw that, and sent her brother with the message because she thought I'd understand it.'

In the silence that followed, Rory sensed that all eyes were on him, and it needed an effort to remain still. The slightest movement would betray him.

'And do you understand it?' Ana persisted, not entirely convinced.

The passageways of gull and shark

Dendroger seemed reluctant to go on, but the others were waiting.

'The great bird, as it calls itself here, is the one that Rory told you about. First, it flies from a boy's kite, then it puts itself above the rest of the world, so that we have to look up to it. It's trying to frighten us; isn't that plain to anyone!'

Now it was the turn of Lars Guonda.

'It would be plainer if we knew how this bird fits into what you've been telling us. You said that the *Book of Mystic Transformations* that Maddy found explains how to change from one creature to another. You say that whoever does this can live for ever, and that we'll be able to do so when we find the fossil shaped like a shoe.'

'Yes, yes,' said Dendroger impatiently. 'The writer of the book made this clear, and is almost certainly still alive in some form or other.'

'Do you mean,' asked Ana, 'that he's taken the form of this bird?'

'It is probably so.' The scowling figure was being pressed to admit more than he had intended; but if he was to keep the others' co-operation, he would have to humour them and appear to take them into his confidence.

'The writer of the book is master of all changes. He can take the form of any living thing he pleases – bird or fish, animal or insect. The passageways of the wind and sea, and the corridors of the deep earth are open to him, as they are to the gull and shark, and to the wolf and moth and mole. He can slip in and out of their natural elements just as it suits him. So he could well be the great bird that the lines refer to.'

Rory could hardly believe his ears. Was he dreaming? Were such amazing things possible? All he had seen and heard in the past months tumbled through his mind in confusion as he thought of what Dendroger had said. Behind him he could distinguish faint sounds as the crab moved about among the debris in the hearth, and he shuddered lest he should be in its path when it blundered from hiding.

Ana was talking.

'As soon as we find the fossil, we'll be able to do these things too. Perhaps the bird is warning us of possible dangers.'

'More likely he is trying to stop us getting the fossil,' lied Dendroger, thinking fast to avoid giving any hint of his own recent experiments, or of his plan to seize all power for himself. 'It's this boy the bird is interested in. The message was meant to lead him here so that he could learn our secrets and be the first to find the fossil. Then we should lose the advantage we have.'

Rory sensed in Dendroger's quick suspicion a hint that he himself was hiding something from the others. What dark, private intrigue was behind his words? The boy could not imagine, but already he was sure that any danger he was in came from the old man.

For the time being however, it seemed that the three were convinced by the argument put forward, and in the whispered conversation that followed, they apparently agreed on what to do. Inwardly, he pictured the grim features of Lars and Jens, and the shifting squint of Ana. The air about him, as he lay on the hard floor, tingled with conspiracy. But against whom? He did not know. Clearly, though, he was in greater peril than he at first supposed. Stiffness and cold were beginning to worry him. His limbs ached, but he dared not show any sign of having stirred. Then with rising panic, Rory heard one of the four approach him, and Dendroger suddenly spoke from right above.

'This boy threatens our plans. We must put him out of the way.'

'Can't we just let him go?' appealed Ana, afraid of what Dendroger might do. 'You could have made a mistake about him.'

'You'll see if I've made a mistake,' snapped back the other. 'Who do you think is the "youngest" that the words speak of? Who is the youngest in the crofts?'

'As it happens, it's Torquil, child of Morag,' said Ana defensively.

'But who is the youngest of the Chefennec family? It's this boy.' Rory felt a sandal nudge his side. 'This boy is old Chefennec's last heir on earth. Listen to me. You saw nothing strange that he made a kite, although such a thing was never heard of in the crofts before. You thought nothing of the fact that the cloth he made it from was decorated with an eagle. You made fun of his story that the kite came alive as a bird just like the one shown on it. Yet when the kite returned to earth, the eagle design was gone: the bare cloth is there to see! Now we have this message that followed it down from the sky.

Look, the writing is the same as that in the book – the same hand that signed the last page: Old Chefennec. He was the great bird that flew from the kite. It's he who is trying to communicate with the boy.'

7

Stairway to the Inner Earth

The stunned silence was only momentary, then all three were speaking at once. Rory's thoughts were racing, as his kite had done across the sky. He still could not believe the full meaning of Dendroger's words: one of Rory's own family had been the first adventurer in those unknown kingdoms, and had written the *Book of Mystic Transformations*. Someone was alive today and had tried to get in touch with him! Had Ailsa guessed all the time? But she had trusted Dendroger. What would she think now if she knew all that had been going on? By some means, he must get away and tell her.

Further thoughts vanished, Dendroger was leaning closer.

'Old Chefennec is playing to get this boy. I believe

he's using him to steal our secret for his own ends.'

To hear one of his own family accused like this made Rory flush with indignation. He felt his mouth tighten, and, too late, realised that the movement had been noticed.

'Ah, the whelp's awake!'

A rough grip jerked at his arms and pulled him to his feet. Involuntarily, he drew back from the ring of fierce faces.

'How long have you been listening? Answer me, boy! What did you hear?'

Rory knew, as the seconds passed, that his own silence accused him. But, come what might, he would tell these people nothing they wanted to know. As long as he kept quiet, he had an advantage of some kind over them. What it was, he did not understand, only that there was a weakness in their schemes, and that they were afraid he had discovered it. He had stumbled on a dark conspiracy: his family and friends might be in danger if he did the wrong thing.

Suddenly Lars lunged forward and caught him by the shoulder.

'Speak up! You heard the question!' he growled.

All of them were waiting: Dendroger, grey as the parched sea holly, his pale eyes not moving from the boy; Ana Guonda, watchful and silent; her husband, breathing heavily; Jens Shardolf, sinewy and agile under his loose clothes. What chance did he have against them? And what would happen if their questions turned to blows, or worse? He wished Ailsa were with him. She was cleverer than most people in the crofts, and had got out of difficult situations before. Yet what could Ailsa do? At least she was still safe outside. If only he could reach the door and make for the safety of the Carp! His glance must have followed his thoughts, for Dendroger read them.

'There's no way out there, boy.'

The great lock looked more unwieldy than ever. Even if he got to the door, he would never turn the key in time.

The window? That was too small and high.

He would have to think of a way of tricking them to catch them off guard. But what? All kinds of crazy possibilities went round in his head, but only seemed to confirm the hopeless trap he was in. With more assurance than he felt, he faced them defiantly.

'One day, I'll be bigger than any of you. Then you wait and see!'

A frightening grin began to tighten the dry skin across Dendroger's face. His long arms reached forward as though to encircle Rory: but, as the boy shrank back from their odious embrace, they stiffened suddenly, stretched out on either side of him, and the old man started cackling. The noise seemed to rattle inside the toothless head, making it nod and sway with almost idiot rhythms. The other three were gazing at him in bewilderment. From the commanding presence of a moment before, he had become transfigured into a pathetic imbecile. It was as if the great weight of years upon him crumbled at a touch, and toppled his senses with them. Then, as quick again, and before anyone had recovered from the shock, the inane laughter stopped abruptly, and the spasm was past. For a moment, the new sense of power had deserted him, but it returned and the voice continued, firm and rational, as though the outburst had never happened.

'It doesn't matter that he won't talk. I've a better use for him. As long as we hold him, we have a weapon against the Chefennecs. If they attempt to interfere, this boy will suffer. We must hide him well. I sense unusual pressures around the house: already, the others are planning how they can rescue him. Unlike themselves, he's still only mortal and can come to harm. They'll do everything in their power to get him away from danger.'

The room had grown dark now. Through the small window, Rory could see the late evening sky, starless and cold. The whisper of night flyers came every so often to his trained ears, and once he saw the ghost swift-moth carried by its curious rocking flight across the opening. Then it was gone. He heard the far-off sea sliding on shingle. All around him outside was the world he knew – a world where haunted companies were astir among the shadows of the Carp, and the velvet air was brushed by the bodies of silent hunters. Everything was going on as usual: the last calls of the bittern and curlew would be sounding from beyond the Grettel marshes, and a rustle in the reeds would tell where a moorhen went into the moonless stream, sending ripples across the slow flow of water. Everything would be the same, but he was not part of it. He was a prisoner, cornered like a vole by weasels.

No one had seen him come or knew he was there except Ailsa; and what could she do? The four might keep him as long as they wished and deny ever having set eyes on him. Where would they take him? There were few places not visited by the crofters, and the children knew every hidden cave for miles. There was nowhere except far away on the moor where the villagers never went.

All at once, he was seized by Lars and Jens, and his arms were tied fast behind him with thick cord smelling of tar and fish. As Jens stooped to pass rope round his legs, he kicked out with all his force, catching the man off-balance and sprawling him on the floor. The grasp on his shoulders hardened instantly, and Lars thrust him to the ground, holding him there till the other had done the job. With a strip of old sacking, Ana Guonda bandaged his eyes. The pressure made the blackness dance with violet and orange lights.

He no longer felt afraid, just utterly alone, as though sealed in one of the ancient burial mounds he had seen uncovered during peat cutting on the slopes overlooking Dollom moor. There was nothing he could do but fight back the outrage at work within him. He tensed, as hands lifted him bodily off the floor.

From the odour of herring nets, he knew that it was Jens Shardolf who carried him, slung across a shoulder. He heard the clang of iron, and the grating of a heavy stone slab. Then he was going down, borne on a jolting motion that indicated steep steps. Down and down he went, the air becoming colder and damper. A giddy feeling, made acute by his blindness, told him that the stairs had begun to wind. The sudden lurch each time his bearer slipped seemed to plunge them both momentarily into a sickening drop through space.

After a while Rory found himself counting the steps, although he reckoned they already numbered several hundred. Now it was another hundred. Then another. The air was so cold by this time that it hurt to breathe. His whole body was aching and shivering. Through his tunic, he could feel Jens's hands loosen their grip now and again to ease the cramp. Progress was slower now and each step seemed an ordeal, for strong though the fisherman was, the freezing dark and the weight across his shoulders were beginning to tell. As Rory's count was approaching the fifth hundred, the bandage slipped from his eyes, and he noticed that the narrow shaft down which they had come was widening and they were descending into a gloomy, domed chamber. On the five hundredth stair exactly, they stopped, and Shardolf, shaking from exertion, dropped his burden on to the ground with a final grunt.

The thud made Rory gasp with pain, and he remained unable to move for several seconds, but the sound of Jens's boots mounting the stairs again made him twist and peer up into the dark. With unbelieving horror, he realised that he was to be left bound hand and foot in that awful pit.

Jens departed without a word, his shadowy form quickly swallowed into the impenetrable darkness overhead. The scrape of his footsteps became fainter;

then he was gone, and silence settled as in a tomb.

Rory stared frantically around. For all he could make out, he was in a void without shape or size. With no object visible by which to get a bearing, his senses began to drift and float, as though rolled on the swell of a night sea. His struggles caused him to rock from side to side, and with an effort, he managed to work across the floor a short distance, ending almost immediately against a wall. By working slowly back again, he found himself against one opposite. Whichever direction was explored, he soon encountered cold stone. There was little doubt that he was in a small cell, overhung by the towering hollow shaft of the stairway. Around was almost total darkness, bearing down from above and pressing in from the sides. Neither sight nor hearing could pick up the faintest trace of anything beyond. Then, from far up came the almost inaudible sound of the trap-door being dropped into place again. Silence flowed back like black water flooding a well and he felt his heart pounding as if it would burst the restraining ropes. He was alone in some secret chamber of the inner earth, deeper than anyone would ever come to look for him.

The thought brought sudden tears to his eyes – he might never again see the sunny hills above, or the sea divided by Carp Point, or Ailsa and the wild things of the woods and the shore. Bright mornings and storm-filled skies reached down and touched his unseeing eyes, so that flowery meadows rose and fell across his blindness, and white tides flowed up to him, and the badger and fox and hare came, and sea birds drifted through the dark, and the phantom calls of all his lost world carried to him through the noiseless air, crying like unreal voices in a dream.

Then into the dream there came a single sound that, instead of fading as the others did, persevered . . . softly, repeatedly, until its presence began to still all unreal ones. The knowledge made him stiffen and he listened, breathless. A small scuffing and creaking, like dried heather in a sack, grew more and more insistent, accompanied now and then by dull, metallic knocks. At first it seemed to come from above in the brooding vault, then nearer, closer to him. As he strained to hear better, something touched him. Though bound, he jerked involuntarily away, and with a gasp of alarm, attempted to put himself beyond its reach. But again it touched, exactly as before, and he realised that the thing was not only close, it was in his pocket!

He craned his head, waiting helplessly for it to emerge. It was trying to free itself from the folds of the material. The efforts became rhythmic and increasingly violent until, without warning, it broke from cover and clambered off him on to the ground.

Glowing phosphorescent, the giant claws of the crab swayed smoothly from side to side as the creature regarded the boy with its polished eyes. Then, raising itself to its full height, it moved along him as though skirting a rock until level with his startled face. Never before had Rory been afraid of these hunters of the tides, but as he looked into the small mask and the deadly weapons swinging before it, he remembered the way

It broke from cover and clambered off him on to the ground

they browsed day and night to satisfy their hunger; he remembered them pouring in multitudes through the waves, devouring as they went, fastening on to whatever washed past. He wrenched his head aside and, with wild desperation, twisted to try and loosen the cords, but they chafed through his coarse clothing and held securely. He was at the mercy of the thing beside him.

So this was the fate that Dendroger had planned for him – to be left as prey for this scavenger of the seas! But he would put up a fight. He still had power to kick out with both legs together. If necessary, he would roll on the creature and smother it. At all costs, he must avoid the slashing claws.

Then suddenly, they disappeared. Alert for what might happen, he was surprised by a sharp snapping noise behind his back. Over his shoulder he saw the crab attacking the rope that held his wrists. With calculated and precise movements, the pincers were sawing and cutting at the strands by turn. The sight of the owner so bent to the work, filled him with astonishment. He watched as the frayed ends slowly parted and the first rope fell clear.

During the next few minutes, one after another of the coils gave way before the crab's exertions, and soon Rory was able to help by loosening and untying the rest. Numbed and sore, he got unsteadily to his feet.

The crab was still standing looking at him, and Rory remembered how it had nestled in the great hand of Jens Shardolf and allowed itself to be stroked. It belonged to his enemies: why had it done this for him? Had one of the four smuggled it into his pocket for that purpose? But no; they had all been against him. The stowaway must have crept there of its own accord, unnoticed. His first mistrust began to fade, and he was about to bend and pick it up when a sudden chill swept through him. A new and different sound was vibrating softly in the darkness. The chamber filled with a quiet breathing that could have been his own or another's nearby. He would have turned and run, but there was nowhere to run to; and then, the sound was a voice repeating his name. The single word echoed round the hollow walls, but in the intense gloom, Rory could see no one.

8

Encounter in the Buried Forest

'Rory!'

The voice, sounding at first from everywhere around him, seemed to draw closer.

'Rory, listen carefully. You don't know me, but you needn't be afraid. Although you were sent to Dendroger's house, I was there to make sure you didn't come to harm. You have heard folk talk of your grandfather, old Chefennec, and of how he left the crofts a long time ago with his brothers. I am Rognvald Chefennec, one of those brothers. I lived once in the old stone cottage on the edge of Grettel marshes where I collected reeds and canes from the beds for weaving into crab pots. I knew all there was to know about the craft, but since then, I've learned a far greater one.

'As you heard in the room above, your grandfather developed an amazing skill. He passed this on to his brothers, and now, like him, we can take the likeness of any creature, and live wherever it lives itself.

'Look down, Rory: my armoured back and big claws needn't deceive you as they've deceived others tonight.'

Rory stared in disbelief at the crab which still watched him from the floor. It showed no sign of having spoken, and Rory wondered if he had imagined the incident; but the voice went on.

'As a crab, I can't talk to you: there are some laws that bind even us. But I can do so from my presence within the crab's shape. One day you'll see clearly why we had to do these things, and how we are extending life into new regions. Your grandfather hoped that others would learn the secret in time, and he left a book as a guide for them – the one which Maddy Obdolon found. Unfortunately, it fell into the wrong hands. We know Dendroger of old, and were lads with him long ago: he was a wicked one, even then. He came to know that we had made important experiments, and when the book turned up in Maddy's hands, he recognised at once that it was a record of them, although he pretended not to. From that moment, we foresaw that he'd be up to no good and would use the book for his own ends. So we never let him out of sight: it's as easy to be a ghost swift-moth as it is to be a crab!'

With a start, Rory remembered the small window in the room above and the white shape that had fluttered past. It was reassuring to think that he had not been quite alone up there.

'Ingvar Chefennec was that moth,' the voice continued. 'From window sill and lampshade, he watched Dendroger struggling with the secret of the book so that he could try out the immense power it would give him. If he succeeded, the crofts would be in danger, and later perhaps, the whole world.

'We hoped at first that he wouldn't be able to understand the instructions for changing into other creatures, but after a few days it was clear he was on the right track and near to doing so. So we thought it best to show our hand and let him know we were around. It might deter him, knowing that he had to deal with us if he got up to mischief. So Sigurd Chefennec changed into a dog-fox and purposely laid a scent for the croft mongrels to pick up. Their barking was meant to rouse the village so that everyone would see, but no one paid attention, and the dogs got too close for comfort. In the end, it was only Morag who saw the fox change – just in time, as it happened; although her screams would have put the dogs to flight even if the wolf hadn't. At least they made everyone come running to find out what had happened!

'Unfortunately, Dendroger had shut himself away, and the news didn't reach him: so we had to do something else that he was bound to hear of. Jens Shardolf was one of the few people who visited the house, with his usual deliveries of shellfish. So this time, Torquil Chefennec swam out with the herring shoal and, while Jens was watching, changed into a shark at the moment the gannet dived. Luckily the timing was good, because as a result, the trawl went overboard and the boat struck the Jak, so that Jens had plenty of evidence to back up his story and was sure to tell it well.

'The news reached Dendroger next day but only seemed to spur him on, and we saw that he'd succeed before the night was out. It was this that made us decide to meet and see what could be done.'

Rory was listening spellbound to the tale being unfolded. He had forgotten that he could not see the speaker; he had forgotten the cold and his own danger. From time to time, he glanced at the crab, but it remained motionless as before, and might just as well have been asleep for all the part it was taking in the conversation. Rory found a strange comfort in the confident tone of the voice, but could not help feeling a little uneasy that he had put his whole trust in a crab. He looked anxiously upward in the direction of the stairway, fearing that Jens or one of the others would come down and find that he had got free. But there was no sound from above, no step on the stairs. Then the revelations continued.

'That meeting, Rory, was the one you walked into on your way home across the marsh. We were all there except Ingvar, who stayed behind to keep an eye on Dendroger. We had flown as birds to meet on a deserted stretch, and were about to take human shape so that we could discuss the matter freely, when you turned up. That was the first time we'd tried getting back into human form. There had never been need to do so before, and it proved more difficult than we thought: we'd been out of it too long. You came on us at the change-over when we were neither bird nor man. Our first thought was to stop and warn you, but it was too much to expect that you'd understand, so we made off as we were without scaring you further.'

Then he did not imagine it, Rory consoled himself: it really was true after all.

'We arrived at the Carp to learn that Dendroger had completed the experiment. Our worst fear now was that the old rogue would go on to unravel the fateful chapter at the end of the book. We knew the awful outcome that would follow if he did, and Old Chefennec left at once to make a last desperate attempt to prevent it happening. If Dendroger discovered the secret of the mine, all would be lost. The danger was appalling, and every minute wasted meant the difference between life and death.

'First, with the help of powerful friends, he hid the only remaining entrance to the mine on the off-shore islands. You yourself saw them turn the South Jak to do this. Then he decided to send Dendroger a warning that he couldn't ignore by giving you the kite message to take to him. In the shape of a spider, he boarded your kite and, with his own silk, wrote the message on it as it climbed the sky. Then he changed into an eagle, tore off the corner of the kite and, drawing the gold thread of the design after him, flew away. The wind carried the bare kite off, but the message fluttered down to you.'

Rory gasped to think how, without knowing it, he had been caught up in these strange events.

'There was a risk, but we didn't let you go alone. Dendroger had told the three others to bring a hen, a stoat and a crab, which he said they'd need for carrying out the magic process. So, when the beach was deserted, I nestled down as a crab inside the wicker trap that Jens had set, and was taken to Dendroger's house along with the hen and stoat that you passed on the Carp.'

Despite his predicament, Rory grinned at the thought of Jens carrying the 'enemy' into his own camp without realising it.

'Inside the house, I watched Dendroger rehearse the others in the foolish pantomime designed to lure them on to the final stage – finding the fossil in the mine. With it once in his hands, Dendroger treacherously planned to drop his accomplices and use the fossil to gain complete control for himself. Then you arrived, and he saw how he could keep you as hostage to make the Chefennecs do what he wanted them to. I managed to stow away in your jacket before they tied you up and brought you here. The job now is to get you out. These walls are very thick and I'll have to go for help. Any time after I've left, watch for the first chance to escape and then move fast.'

With this, the crab seemed to come to life, and started examining round the bottom of the wall, feeling hastily over the stonework with its claws. At a point where the cement had weakened, it set to work scratching more away until there was a space large enough to crawl through. As the crab disappeared between the stones and came up against the packed earth on the other side, Rory glimpsed the hard form soften to a black velvet one and change shape at the same moment that the claws contracted to become paddle shaped hands. Within seconds, a mole was shovelling upwards and had vanished.

Rory stared at the hopelessly narrow opening. The heavy slabs would have to be loosened and pulled away if he were to squeeze through; and even then he would still be several hundreds of feet underground. Only a mole could tunnel up through solid earth. As the silence continued around him and nothing happened, he wondered how soon it would be before he heard the trap door being raised far above and the sound of footsteps descending the stairs. Yes, there it was! His heart beat faster as he caught the noise – the scrape of boots on stone. Someone was coming down to the cellar. What was he to do? He thought quickly of lying down and pretending that he was still tied up; then, before he could make a move, he realised that the scraping was outside the wall, and not coming from above.

The stones on either side of the opening made by the crab were starting to move. Through the crack appeared a round, fleshy point like the cap of a mushroom. As it intruded inch by inch into the cellar, it swelled, forcing the two stones further apart. With each advance it became bigger, widening the aperture still more until, under pressure from the slowly expanding form, the stones swung inwards and toppled to the floor. The sudden action caused the plant to drop, exposing behind it a long tunnel through which the thick stem had been working its way. It was coming from the direction which the mole had taken, and could have been the same tunnel much enlarged by the thrusting plant. Loose falls of earth continued to open up the height of the tunnel and, remembering the crab's advice, Rory stepped over the mushroom head and, bent nearly double, scrambled back along the course it had been taking.

At times, there was barely room to squeeze through and he had to clear some of the surrounding soil before he could proceed. The way led slightly uphill, and Rory pulled himself along by hauling on the tendril, whose progress in the opposite direction had slowed down and was now almost stopped. In the dark, he felt the plant becoming harder and thicker – more like the root of a tree. His hands followed it as it continued gradually upwards and overhead to a height above him that he could not reach. It was the first he knew of having come out of the tunnel into an enlarged space. He could now stand erect and, by a pale green glow that was lightening the gloom, he saw that the root he had been following was one of many curving up from all sides into the roof of what was a vast underground cavern. Like arches, they soared to meet each other at a point far above, and in the eerie light, he became aware of more clusters of arches beyond, forming a maze of aisles receding one behind the other into the distance. As far as he could see in all directions, the whole area was vaulted by giant overhanging roots that came down through the earth above. Soil had long ago fallen away from between them, leaving spacious cavities and creating a sub-

The whole area was vaulted by giant overhanging roots

terranean world faintly illuminated by phosphorescent lichens and mosses that spread a carpet underfoot. He remembered stories he had been told of the ancient coal forest that had lain buried for millions upon millions of centuries below the Carp, and realised that he must have emerged underneath its floor.

A closer examination of the tree roots showed that many had put out curious growths such as the one he had followed, each feeling its way through a crack in the surrounding wall as though trying to probe beyond it. Was a dead forest still searching for life? Had the mole's tunnel opened a way for a root to explore it and so break through into Rory's prison? That would explain why it stopped soon after entering, for there was nothing of value inside!

With a start, he recalled the mole. What had become of it? He could still not bring himself to believe all that had happened. Had the crab really changed into the mole and helped him to escape? If so, where was the mole now?

Rory looked around but could only make out shapes here and there of what appeared to be enormous bulbs pushing up through the moss. They were scaled like fir cones, and sprouted ferny fronds from the top; but all were turned to stone. If there was life overhead in the forest, there was little enough in this grotesque garden underneath. Nothing moved or made a sound. Rory wondered why the mole should have brought him safely out of one trap to abandon him in another. All ways looked the same: there was nothing for it but to keep on along one of them until the path began to rise again, as his main aim must be to get back to the surface somehow. For a while he followed the straightest of the tunnels to a point where it became lost among others branching off from it. Confused by the flowing line of the roots that rose and fell on all sides, he was never sure whether he was going up or down, and despaired of ever finding a likely exit.

All at once, the route ahead was blocked by a sheer barrier of earth stretching to left and right. He was about to turn back, thinking he had come to a dead end, when he noticed that a small section of the wall near the ground had caved in, leaving a gap just big enough to admit him. Crawling through, he found himself in total darkness, and had barely time to adjust to it after the pale green glow of the tunnels behind, when another yellower glow appeared in the distance. As it approached it swayed, as though being carried, and by its light Rory made out the shapes of four figures advancing along the low-roofed corridor which he had entered.

His joy at finding that he was not alone was overtaken by sudden panic as he recognised the shrill tones of one of the figures and heard the growled response from a second. Instinctively, he drew back into the shadow of the opening as Dendroger, a lantern in his hand, passed within a few steps of where he hid. Behind the old man trailed Lars with his wife Ana, and Jens Shardolf, the fisherman. The watcher's heart pounded as he saw them looking this way and that, peering into the gloom. What were they doing here? Had they discovered he was missing and come to search for him? But there had been no sounds of a pursuit, and either way the four had come from the opposite direction. Somehow they must have descended into the underground vaults from the other end of the Carp.

He watched until the group had gone some way along the gallery, their shadows dancing behind as the light shook; then cautiously, and keeping as close to the wall as possible, he followed at a safe distance behind. He could see that they were in a natural passage that had been shored at intervals to prevent any collapse of the walls and roof. These were of some kind of compressed mud, blue and grey in colour, and studded here and there with curiously formed shapes. Could this be the long lost mine that he had heard so much about? With new excitement, he glanced again at the shapes embedded in the walls, thinking how much they resembled the shells and forms of living creatures. But these were frozen in the stillness of death. He had just time to notice how perfectly they were preserved when, with a suddenness that nearly made him pitch forward, he realised that the group ahead had stopped and were standing round the lantern in the centre of the ring of shadows. Dendroger's shrill cry went echoing along the empty labyrinths, breaking in on the ageless silence of the earth.

'There!' he piped, his thin, grotesque figure making the shadows reel. 'The fossil of eternal life!'

In his hand, he held the fossil trilobite, its ridged body shaped remarkably like a shoe.

9

The Voice of the Eagle

From where he stood in the shadows, Rory thought that
the object which Dendroger had picked up from the clays
did not look much to be excited about; but the old man
clutched it possessively and winding his cloak around
him, started back along the passage with the others at his
heels. Rory returned quickly to the gap in the wall and
waited until they had gone by; then, when they were far
enough ahead, he slid from hiding and followed.

For most of the time the passage ran straight, and he
kept the silhouetted figures in sight; but now and then
it turned a corner, and all he had to go by was the last of
the light as it disappeared. There was no doubt now in
Rory's mind that he had struck the course of the lost
mine, and he could imagine Old Chefennec and his
brothers at work here long ago, digging for the treasure
they hoped to find.

The ground was rising by stages and, after a while, began to climb more steeply. The four in front had said hardly a word, and it was clear that Dendroger was hurrying them on. At last they came to a heavy, unlocked door, which they opened and passed through. Beyond was a narrow flight of steps, lit with early morning sunshine that streamed from above. Not troubling to close the door, they mounted the stairs and, giving them time to get clear, Rory went up after them. The opening led out on to a platform of rock overhung by a projecting ledge. Keeping well down, he took in the scene at a glance and, with mixed surprise and alarm, saw that they had emerged under the seaward side of the South Jak.

Dendroger and his party, with anxious looks around and obviously eager to be away, were clambering into Jens's boat, tied up alongside a boulder. The fisherman pushed off and rowed round the island, making with all his might for Carp Point.

As the boat with its occupants dwindled into the distance, Rory stared across the channel to the mainland. Normally the idea of being stranded alone on the sinister rock would have horrified him, but he was so glad to be out from underground and rid of his four enemies that his first feelings of dismay vanished. But how was he to get back to the Carp? For a change the sea was calm, but he had never attempted to swim such a distance and, against the strong cross currents, doubted if he would ever make it.

He explored the small island and discovered that its

whole upper mass was naturally pivoted in a shallow saucer of rock below sea level. So that was how it was turned! But what inconceivable strength could have done it? His mind filled with all the vague fears and superstitions to which the incident had given rise and he had to take hold of himself to prevent them overpowering him again.

The boat had reached nearly half way across the channel when a sudden shadow fell upon the island. Looking up, Rory saw the shape of a large bird, dark against the sun. The spread of the vast wings brought back an instant picture of his kite eagle; and then, with a joy he could not explain, he knew it was the same! Barely altering its poise, the great bird lowered itself on to a pinnacle overhead, composed and motionless, its eyes fixed on the boy. Rory knew without questioning that he was in the presence of Old Chefennec himself.

The voice that drifted down through the still air was calm and deep, and although the curved beak did not move, Rory took it for granted that he need look for no other speaker.

'Rory, you're young to find yourself among so many strange events and facing such dangers. But you're a Chefennec, and I'm proud of my grandson. I hoped, one day, that I might return to you in a form you'd know, but I'm afraid the time is passed and it may never be. It is possible, however, that I shall soon have news for you of another sort. But for now, I'm glad you're safe. Rognvald was worried when he went back to guide you out of the escape tunnel from Dendroger's cellar and found you'd gone. Did you see anything of the Giants Gonby and Bygon?'

'Who are the Giants Gonby and Bygon?' stammered Rory, only too relieved to think he had not had giants to deal with as well.

'They're the Coal Masters who live underground in the buried forest. Rognvald went to them and asked them to help get you out of the prison, and they despatched one of the foraging roots from their trees to break in and release you. They use these roots for bringing back what they need from the deeper earth.'

'Then it was the giants who saved me!' said Rory.

'Just as they saved me,' replied the voice from the eagle. 'You know of the process I discovered that makes it possible to change into the forms of other creatures. Afterwards, I learned a secret more difficult to believe. I had only to stand in the shoe-shaped fossil, and I could go back to the beginning of Time and be safe even from the destroying powers of fire and ice and the crushing weight of the earth. It was down in the mine where you've just been that I finally found the fossil. To think how near I was to a terrible fate! Even now, I tremble to recall the narrow escape I had.

'I closed the land entrance of the mine from underground, hid the record of my discoveries, and returned through the underground galleries to the exit we'd left open on the South Jak. With the fossil in my hand, I took a wrong turn and found myself unexpectedly in the cavern of the Giants, a world of its own contained within the forest and completely new to me. My immediate fear on meeting them proved to be unfounded, for they showed only friendliness until I told them of my intentions. When they saw the fossil trilobite, their good humour turned to deep concern, and they warned me in most solemn and awful tones to have nothing to do with it. "You are correct," they said, "in thinking that you can go back through the infernos of Time by standing in the fossil, but what you cannot know is that you will never come back again! You will be stranded for all eternity on the far shores of Creation and never set foot on the paths of life again. Nothing will ever be heard of you for as long as the universe lasts."'

Rory gasped as he tried to imagine the fearful consequences.

'When I learned that Dendroger had discovered the secret of the fossil from the last part of my book,' the eagle went on, 'I at once asked the Giants to help me again by turning the South Jak so that the entrance to the mine was concealed. Evil though he is, I wouldn't wish him the fate that awaits anyone who finds the fossil and puts it to use. For his sake, I hope he never finds the entrance.'

The full realisation of what the eagle was saying broke on Rory like a shattering wave. He stared across the water to where the small boat was just drawing in to the far headland.

'But Dendroger has already found the entrance and taken away the fossil!' He pointed towards the tiny group of figures in the distant boat. 'He's over there now

He pointed towards the tiny group of figures in the distant boat

with Lars and Ana and the fisherman. They're on their way home to carry out the final experiment!'

With a sharp twist of its fine head, the eagle followed the direction in which Rory pointed. A ripple ran through the folded wings and, turning for the briefest moment to the boy as though to reassure him, it lifted clear of the rock and climbed steadily into the blue air towards the Carp. Rory gazed after it until the bright distance and the sparkling sea dazzled him and he had to look away. Glancing from one Jak to the other nearby, he wondered why it was that they appeared in some way to be different.

10

Doom of the Trilobite

With the beach only a stone's throw away, Dendroger was congratulating himself. From the moment he had guessed about the South Jak, he was sure that the mine entrance was concealed under a low shelf of rock barely above water level. It had been important to have good weather for finding it, and luck had been with him. The morning sea was flat and calm, and before anyone to his knowledge was astir in the crofts, he and his accomplices had pulled out to the island and located the steps leading to the mine. It had taken only minutes for Lars to unlock the door at the bottom, and their search of the underground gallery had led them almost straight to the fossil beds where they found what they were after. Only the false promise he had made to the other three gave them courage to face the unknown perils of the Jak; and he was glad he would soon be rid of them.

As the keel grounded on the shingle of Carp Point, they waded ashore, and while Dendroger flapped impatiently around them, the others pulled the boat on to the beach. The old villain had no further use for them and would like to have left them there and then; but to avoid arousing their suspicions, he must let them think that they were still all working together. His plan was to set up some foolish stage effects at home, intended as a prelude to the magic rite, then tell them to return at the correct hour of midnight in order to carry it out. Long before then, however, he would have completed his experiment with the fossil and be in a position of absolute command to do as he wished.

A short way up the shingle bank he waited, holding tight to his precious trophy and exhorting them to make haste. It was then that he happened to glance up at the sky and see the dark shape approaching. One moment he was about to dismiss it as of no importance, the next, he froze in his antics as though turned to marble. In that instant, and by some instinct that needs no proof, he had recognised in the powerful span the great bird of the kite – and his sworn opponent, Old Chefennec. As the wings above him lifted and tensed, and the smooth body streaked earthwards to seize the fossil in its steel grip, Dendroger was jerked to life by a single, blind impulse – to take the one step that would put him beyond the reach of the avenging claws. Crazed by his desire for total power, and in panic that it could be wrested from him, he set the fossil on the ground and, fitting his shoe exactly in it, stood upright, his eyes fast shut, willing it to discharge its mystic energy and take him back through Time.

What the other three witnessed from lower down the slope, they were never to forget to their dying day, nor be able to tell to another living soul without trembling at the recollection. As the rush of heavy wings swept past from overhead, aimed at the solitary figure poised above them like a statue, the whirl of feathers was checked suddenly by a spear of intense blue light that enveloped the old man and shrank, extinguished, into an incandescent glow among the pebbles. In the spot where Dendroger had stood a second earlier, lay only the fossil, rocking slightly as though some weight had sprung from it; and then the huge bird was regaining height from its plunge and climbing towards the sky.

They remained, gazing at the empty beach, unable to grasp what had happened. Turning to each other in consternation, they looked first at the place where the old man had been, then at the eagle, circling high above them and seemingly distressed. Before they could recover themselves, the bird, as though making a second attempt, dived again and gathered up the fossil, bearing it out to sea. In the off-shore deeps, they saw the white splash as the object dropped into the water and vanished for ever under the waves.

Ana was the first to come to her senses and, with a woman's intuition, realised that in some way Dendroger had cheated them, and had foiled even Old Chefennec at the final throw.

'He knew more than he let on,' she said to the others.

Where Dendroger had stood lay only the fossil, rocking slightly

'He never meant to share his secret with us. Once we'd got the fossil for him, he was finished with us. Just playing us along, he was!'

'Reckon you were right after all,' mumbled Jens Shardolf. 'The kite bird was trying to warn us, not to threaten as the old fellow made out. Now what's become of Dendroger, I wonder!'

'Whatever's happened, I'm glad we're out of it at last,' Lars growled, for the first time smiling grimly. 'I was never happy, tangled up in that business. There are things as no one should meddle with, and magic's one of them.'

The sound of sliding shingle made them look up sharply. Making her way down the slope was Ailsa, her long hair flying and her wrap hastily thrown on. Breathlessly, she came up to the group at the sea's edge.

'It's Rory!' she gasped. 'He's missing. I waited for him all night to come home and was out at first light trying to find him. There was no one in Dendroger's house, so I searched the Carp right to the Grettel marshes and worked back here to the Point. You must help me. I'm sure he's in terrible danger somewhere.'

Her plea moved each of the three to exchange glances of agreement. Ana spoke for the others.

'We do know where he is, Ailsa. Dendroger has played us all false. I'm not ashamed to admit I was in the wrong and went along with him in a devilish scheme he had. But that's all over now, and we must rescue your brother from where the old man hid him.'

The relief that flooded across Ailsa's face changed

suddenly to excitement as, looking seaward past Ana's shoulder, she caught sight of the South Jak, clear in the morning sun. As her expression altered, her neighbours turned and, in utter bewilderment, made out the small figure waving from the distant rock.

Not even attempting to fathom how the boy got there from the cellar under Dendroger's house, the two men launched the boat for the second time that day, and pulled out strongly for the off-shore island. As Ailsa nervously watched her brother scramble aboard, Ana told her all that had occurred, and when the boat returned safely, they ran together into the water to help bring it ashore.

Out to sea a black fin surfaced, gleaming in the sun. It made a wide sweep towards the shore, then veered and sank from view. Nearby, a large crab scurried across the pebbles to a patch of wet sand and, burrowing like a mole, disappeared beneath it. High above an eagle glided past, making for the inland hills, from whose dim retreats the voice of a lone wolf came clear on the morning air. As the blacksmith and his wife, with Jens a step or so behind, followed the brother and sister to their home, a swift-moth fluttered from the gorse and vanished again among the prickly stems. Neighbours joined the party on the way, and by the time they reached the door, a dozen or more had collected, eager to hear the story that was already being rumoured. Boys and girls from the crofts were among them, and more arrived to swell the numbers, until it seemed that all the crofts were gathered in and around the cottage.

As best he could, Rory answered the questions they put to him, explaining all he had come to learn about the strange events of the past few weeks. As the incredible tale unfolded, old and young alike began to feel that the great shadow that overhung the Carp was starting to move away, though many still felt uneasy that a presence they did not understand remained among them. In a way that none could put into words, however, something of the evil had gone out of it, and this feeling was strengthened by reports of latecomers from the Point. For the first time in living memory, sea birds were setting down on the Twin Jaks. From far and wide, gulls and cormorants, gannets and kittiwakes were circling the islands and landing on them to explore the rocks and crannies, like children who had found a new playground. Then Rory knew what it was about the Jaks that had struck him as unfamiliar, and his heart felt suddenly lighter. He wondered sadly what had become of the eagle and the other creatures he had learned to trust. Had they gone forever into a world of their own that he would never glimpse again, or into a past where they, and the roaming spirits in them, rightly belonged? As it happened, Old Chefennec had penned what he thought was the last chapter of his book, but the end was to be written by another hand.

11

The Dream

The night's adventures and all the talk of the morning had left Rory exhausted, so as the afternoon was still fine, he made his way to the western end of the Carp and lay among the high rocks looking out over the sunlit channel to the Twin Jaks.

The flat sea appeared to reflect both the green depths beneath and the cool blue of the sky, as though a mirror were held to each world. It was difficult to believe that far below the placid surface roamed the giants of the sunken forest, whose silence had been broken into by adventurers and thieves. Would they ever rest easy while the back door remained open to their world on the South Jak?

Sleepily, he let his gaze wander beyond the Jaks to the spot where the falling fossil had splashed into the waves. Under how many countless fathoms did it lie submerged, lost to the sight of men? It had travelled a long, hard journey from the beginning of Time, and deserved to be left in peace. His glance lingered on the shining patch of water, and he was lulled by the lift and fall of the gentle swell until a drowsiness overcame him and he drifted slowly into sleep.

As he slept, the light above the place he had been watching began to brighten. A glowing ball of vapour appeared to rise from the sea and, like a giant bubble, floated towards the shore and up the slope. Unable to move, he felt the luminous cloud surround him and his eyes tighten to shut out its glare. As though to a dreamer, the sound of a conversation came to him from within the sphere, and he recognised one of the voices as his own.

'I'm Rory Chefennec,' he was announcing. 'Who are you?'

'I'm the Overseer of Creation,' the other answered.

'The Overseer of Creation?' Rory repeated, at a loss as to what else to say.

'I'm not surprised you don't know me,' the stranger reassured him. 'Since I helped to launch life on the seas of Time, I've been stranded on their remotest shore. Once I'd set things in motion, I was compelled to remain where I was. That was the law. From then on, life had to look after itself until such time as one of its creatures returned to the beginning and opened a channel for me to pass through. Down the ages I've been waiting for this opportunity, because I saw almost as soon as the first forms took shape, that I'd made a mistake. They started interfering with each other in order to survive, and that's not what was intended. They were meant to live and let live. But, once begun, the process couldn't be stopped. I was powerless to intervene, as I wasn't able to break through the barrier of Time and Space to come and help.'

'Then how are you here?' Rory asked, he hoped not rudely.

'Because today such a passage was opened by a mortal from this side. I'm sad for him, of course, since he's alone now on the other edge of Creation, but he has the comfort of being immortal, which apparently is what he wanted. He knows that if he tries to return now, he will age by each million years through which he journeys, and be only a part of the extinct past when he arrives here.'

'But you came through the fossil all right,' Rory ventured.

'I'm not answerable to mortal laws as he is – only to eternal ones. I can now come and go as I please, and will keep a closer eye on matters from now on.'

'What are you going to do?' asked Rory. After events of the past weeks, he was prepared for anything to happen.

'Already,' the Overseer explained, 'intelligent beings have discovered for themselves the secret of a happier existence. The first to do so established their way of life not far from here on the moor. They didn't stray far afield among other folk because no one else was ready for such an advance. A mortal of your own family went to them for help and received it, so that he and his brothers became like them; but unwisely they buried a clue here in the shape of a book. In the wrong hands, it led to trouble, as you know, and they had to come back to try and put things right. This won't happen again. They've returned to the moor with the other beings and will stay there until those left behind learn in their own time. By true age, Old Chefennec and his brothers have exceeded the human life span and can never enter man's form again.'

'But you still don't say what you're going to do,' insisted the boy, astonished at his own audacity.

'Somewhere along the line, life took a wrong turn because it couldn't see beyond what it wanted for itself. I'm going to raise the watch-tower in men's minds so that they'll have more open views and see further across the needs of others. The change must start from them until it broadens to include all manner of life and a better arrangement is found for living together. As present horizons deepen, it will be seen that life exists at all levels of space and time, belonging to a single creation. You yourself have glimpsed below the surface into the vanished world of the coal forests where a different order has made itself at home underground. From the earth's centre to the limits of space, life is active in one shape or another, but not as you know it. You mustn't be surprised to find it as still as rock or light as a breeze. Its pulse may be too slow to feel, its presence too thin to see or too fierce to approach. It moves to a different rhythm from yours, but it's secure within the plan of creation. I admit there have been setbacks; it was a first experiment, after all. But the position isn't out of hand, and everything will find its place in the end.'

'Can't you do anything about the book that caused all the bother?' asked Rory. 'As long as that's around, it'll be a nuisance.'

'That's what I want you to attend to,' confided the Overseer. 'Do as I say, and there'll be no more trouble on the Carp.'

Waking, Rory rubbed his eyes and blinked, as he found himself staring up into the bright sky. He was alone on the ridge – or thought he was until he heard the sound of footsteps behind him. Jens Shardolf was climbing the slope with the book in his hands.

'I've got this from Dendroger's house,' he panted, as he came up. 'I think we ought to get rid of it before it makes more mischief.'

Inspired with a thought, Rory asked Jens if he would row them both out to the South Jak and throw the manuscript overboard.

'It'll only float and come ashore again somewhere else,' objected the fisherman.

'Not where we're putting it,' grinned Rory, secretively. As the boat pulled in to the far side of the island, the passenger leaned over and dropped the cause of all the trouble straight down the entrance to the old mine, where it lay at the bottom of the steep flight of steps. Jens had just pushed away and got clear when they saw the great rock quiver and, with a dull thunder, slip sideways into the sea, blocking for ever the opening to

They saw the great rock slip sideways into the sea

the underworld and leaving its citizens undisturbed. The South Jak lay on its side, a short reach from its twin, and under the evening sun, the birds that had taken to the air and waves, returned and settled down for the night on the two islands.

At home Ailsa had cooked a large pot of potatoes from the clamp, and served them up with butter beans, barley grain and winter spinach. Two apples, stuffed with raisins and spice, were baking in the oven, and two places were set at the table on either side of an earthenware jug containing sprigs of heather.

When Rory burst in, it was more than he could do to wait patiently for Ailsa to put out the meal, but he had a lot to tell her while she did so. Only when they were sitting down together did he notice the kite standing in a corner, with the missing part sewn in place.

'Ana brought it back this afternoon,' his sister explained. 'I mended it with the square of cloth and, as the writing seems to have disappeared, it looks as good as new.

'Ailsa,' Rory said, as the kite reminded him of something, 'do you think we could make a day of it and go to Dollom moor tomorrow?'

'Why should you want to go there?' asked his sister with surprise.

'Well,' replied Rory, toying with a fork, 'for two reasons really: first, because the voice in the dream spoke about it; and second, because of something the eagle said. I've got a feeling that everything isn't over yet, and that the end of the story lies out on the moor somewhere.'

'It's a long way,' warned Ailsa, 'and we wouldn't be back till after nightfall.'

'That won't matter,' Rory said. 'We'll be with each other, won't we.'

Barely visible, it was getting larger

12

On Dollom Moor

Early next morning they set out together for the moor. The clear skies of yesterday had clouded over, but a wintry sun shone through, and as they climbed to the top of the inland hills, Dollom moor stretched out below them into a hazy distance.

The descent was down tracks winding among high pines and matted with dead bracken and briers, but they made good progress and it was not long before they found themselves clear of the woods and in the open country that led on to the moor itself. As far as they could see ahead, the expanse was bare of all except patchy turf, interrupted only by stunted shrubs and small mounds. By midday, with the inland hills well behind, the wilderness had closed around them, and they stopped to eat the scones and cheese that Ailsa had packed for the trip. A further hour's walk brought them to within sight of two huge stones, erected side by side to form a natural archway. They towered from the flat land, joining it to the sky. As Rory and Ailsa stood under them, looking up at the sheer faces of the rock, the stones seemed in motion with the clouds that flowed overhead.

Sheltered between the pillars, they watched the moorland birds gliding to alight in the scrub or take off into the grey wind. Carried to the listeners from among unnumbered voices came the liquid trill of the curlew, and the croak of a hooded crow on course for the estuary. They heard the growling call of a guillemot and from high in the air, the buzzard's lonely mew. At a further height from which no sound reached them, they observed an eagle slowly turn and soar into the empty halls of space.

Rory remembered his encounter on the marsh, and saw again the winged shapes wheel and fly into the dusk; he knew they were at home here where wild creatures live. Like them, he too felt strangely at ease, and looking at Ailsa seated quietly beside him, was sure she understood as he did.

Yet there was something else, something that neither he nor she could explain. The feeling they shared that they were among friends could not be accounted for only by the spirit of the moor. It went deeper, trembling at an untouched chord that had as yet given no sound and waited, expecting to be played. As though by some command that neither admitted to the other, they each kept still, saying nothing and looking out across the moor beyond the pillars of stone. What was it that had moved Rory to suggest coming as far as this, and why had Ailsa agreed to accompany him with no more than a moment's hesitation?

Almost in the same instant, their attention was drawn to a movement in the distance. Barely visible, it was getting larger, until they could make out the shape of some animal. A sudden alarm made Ailsa clutch at her brother's sleeve, and they exchanged quick glances. No, it was too big for a wolf – too big even for one of the moor ponies that they had seen from time to time on the horizon. As the animal altered course for a distance to skirt an area of outcropping rocks, they saw another shape behind it.

'That's a horse and cart!' cried Rory excitedly.

Ailsa's sigh of relief was followed at once by a fresh concern.

'Who would be crossing the moor in this direction? No one that we know comes this way.'

'Perhaps it's a gypsy,' suggested the boy. They had heard of such folk who roamed the outlying countryside, travelling from place to place but never settling.

The horse-drawn cart was near enough now for them to pick out the figure at the reins. No gypsy, certainly, but no one they knew either. Within hailing distance, the driver spotted them and stood up in the cart. He was roughly dressed, his shirt open at the neck and a cape of coarse tweed thrown about his shoulders. Black hair fell across his eyes, which were fixed on the couple by the stones with a look of quiet curiosity.

As he drew up alongside, his eyes never left their faces, and he regarded them earnestly from the stationary wagon, the reins loose in his large hands. The only sound was that of the horse, which had taken advantage of the halt to crop the thin turf. The action jerked the cart forward a pace, and the man called sharply to the culprit without turning.

Then suddenly he smiled.

Ailsa, caught unexpectedly by the changed expression, made a quick curtsey, and Rory grinned. The man's voice was gentler than his appearance would have led to believe.

'What are two youngsters doing so far from home?' he asked. 'You surely can't live under those two stones!'

Rory stepped forward, leaving Ailsa looking on.

'We're just out for the day on the moor,' he said boldly, gazing up into the steady eyes above him. 'We didn't expect to meet anyone.'

'You're from the Carp then, I shouldn't wonder,' guessed the stranger.

'Are you going that way, mister?' the boy asked, without answering the question.

'Maybe I am,' the other volunteered. 'That is, if you'd care to climb aboard and show me the way.'

Rory caught his sister's glance and read the doubt in it.

'Will you tell us who you are, mister, and what your business is at the Carp? We got here by ourselves and can get back the same way if needs be.'

'There's strange things been happening of late, sir,'

Ailsa intervened, thinking her brother may have given offence. 'We have to be careful.'

'It was a wise precaution of the boy's to ask,' the man said, and dropping the reins, he swung himself down from the cart to stand between them.

'Now it's funny you should mention strange things,' he went on, 'because it was a strange thing that brought me here today. Maybe if I tell you, you won't believe; but if I don't, it'll be difficult to answer your questions.

'A few days ago, I was rebuilding a dry-stone wall on grazing slopes some miles away, when a field-lark came and perched on it right beside me. Now that was unusual as you may know, for they're timid birds and don't as a rule come near. It was as though it had deliberately left its own bird world to join me in mine. If I had been surprised by this brave show of friendliness, it was nothing compared with what happened next. In place of the field lark, there appeared beside me the last visitor from the skies I would have expected – a golden eagle!'

Rory and Ailsa looked quickly at each other, then back to the storyteller.

'I see maybe you do believe me,' the man smiled.

'Go on,' stammered Rory, 'what did it say?'

'Well now,' exclaimed the other, 'this is more than I expected. You not only believe me, you know the rest of the story!'

He came close and put his hand on Rory's shoulder, confirming in the boy's expression the likeness he had seen was there.

'Would you, by any chance, be Rory?'

The answering gasp made him turn to face the girl.

'And this, maybe, is Ailsa – grown as pretty as her mother, and no mistake!'

Before the two could reply, the man had his arms round the brother and sister, who made no attempt to resist, but stared from one to the other and back at the unknown traveller between them. Leading them to a rise of ground under the tall stones, he pulled them down beside him.

'Years and years ago, the walls and hedgerows of the crofts were kept in repair by a fellow who lived in a cottage on the south slope. His old father and uncles, the only relatives he had, got mixed up in some kind of magic practice which he disapproved of and would have no part in, though they did invite him to join them. The fellow had a wife and daughter and, after a while, a son.

'Soon afterwards, two blows struck him, one upon the other. First, his wife died unexpectedly; then, going home at night alone after her funeral, he slipped and fell from Carp Point. When he found himself wandering on a moor next day, he could remember nothing. He didn't know who he was, where he came from, or what he was doing there. So he just walked on and on.

'It's a long story, and really doesn't matter: but after several years moving from place to place across the world, taking a job here and a job there, he finally returned to a village not twenty miles from here, and hired himself out mending croft walls. Still he had no recollection of his lost life until the morning when the field-lark changed into an eagle. The shock, I tell you, nearly did for him! But it undid the door to his memory as well, and suddenly everything came flooding back, clear as daylight.'

'And what did the eagle say, mister? You never told us,' Rory blurted out.

'It just said, 'Go home, boy. Ailsa and Rory need their father.'

'You?' cried Rory, 'Our father?'

Ailsa's face was wet with tears as her father's arm tightened around her, and his other clasped a wide-eyed and ecstatic Rory.

'Now maybe I can persuade you to hop in the cart and come home with me,' he smiled.

'Home?' said Rory. 'Yes, let's all go home.'